Gloria continued on up to the fourth floor, but not quite so quickly now. Slowing her progress was the memory of the last time she had climbed these stairs, when all the bad things had started happening.

It was dark up here, with only a wall sconce with three tapered bulbs that gave off little light. Christine must have turned it on.

Standing before the room Hannah had used as her office, Gloria closed her eyes and took a deep breath to still the rush of anxiety she felt building in her chest, but the air up here seemed dead and unbreathable.

In the dark corners of her memory, she could see Eric in his red-and-tan jacket at the open door to the backstairs, and an indistinct shape running from the office. "Here's the joke, Glory," Eric was saying gleefully. "Wait till I tell everybody . . ."

Gloria opened her eyes to see once again a person coming through the doorway.

Panicked, she started to scrabble down the main stairs, unsteady on her Charles Jourdain high heels.

"Mother!" Christine's voice followed Gloria down the stairs.

And then Gloria heard the groan of the elevator as it descended. . . .

By Joyce Christmas
Published by Fawcett Books:

Lady Margaret Priam mysteries:
A FÊTE WORSE THAN DEATH
SUDDENLY IN HER SORBET
SIMPLY TO DIE FOR
A STUNNING WAY TO DIE
FRIEND OR FAUX
IT'S HER FUNERAL
A PERFECT DAY FOR DYING
MOURNING GLORIA

Betty Trenka mysteries:
THIS BUSINESS IS MURDER
DEATH AT FACE VALUE

MOURNING GLORIA

A Lady Margaret Priam Mystery

Joyce Christmas

FAWCETT GOLD MEDAL • NEW YORK

A Fawcett Gold Medal Book
Published by Ballantine Books
Copyright © 1996 by Joyce Christmas

All rights reserved under International and Pan-American Copyright Conventions. Published in the United States by Ballantine Books, a division of Random House, Inc., New York, and simultaneously in Canada by Random House of Canada Limited, Toronto.

http://www.randomhouse.com

Library of Congress Catalog Card Number: 95-90727

ISBN: 0-449-14704-5

Manufactured in the United States of America

First Edition: September 1996

10   9   8   7   6   5   4   3   2   1

For James P. Pray
and
the Irish Wolfhounds of Tucson
personally known to me

Chapter 1

"*Gloria Anton* used to be Gloria Forsythe. She was born a Gilpin," Poppy Dill said in a tone indicating that this explained Gloria once and for all. Her voice on the telephone sounded unexpectedly old and quavery to Lady Margaret Priam. "She's been pretty much out of the New York social mix since her messy divorce from Leland Forsythe. That was at least seven years ago, before you reached our shores, so you wouldn't know her."

Poppy would, however, since she knew everybody, the better to write her "Social Scene" column—now appearing in the newspaper only three times a week in deference both to Poppy's advancing years and to the retreating social parade along the better streets and avenues of Manhattan.

Margaret shifted the receiver to her other ear. "She seems to know me. She's written me a letter about being on a committee."

"Of course people know who you are, even if you don't know them," Poppy said. "A genuine title, and you're quite presentable."

Margaret thought about that for a second. Her title was strictly honorary, the result of being born the daughter of the late Earl of Brayfield. She presumed "presentable" meant that she dressed well, had nice manners, and was widely deemed attractive for a woman in her thirties. Certainly her upper-class British accent was a plus, remaining unaltered for the half dozen or so years she'd been settled in New York.

"Gloria would naturally love to have someone like you for her committee," Poppy said, and lowered her voice confidentially. "She's aiming for a major social comeback, after licking her divorce wounds and having the face-lift, and then marrying that man with the outlandish name."

"Anton? It doesn't sound outlandish to me."

"He calls himself Peter Anton. His real name is something like Antonescu." Poppy paused and then resumed with her customary authority. "That's exactly what it is, Petru Antonescu." Margaret could imagine Poppy rolling her eyes at the very thought, even alone in her fluffy pink boudoir, her aged toes tucked into fluffy pink mules. "A woman like Gloria couldn't go around carrying that burden. The Gilpins were a very fine old New York family. I suppose if Gloria were still a young thing, she might be able to handle it, given the climate of our times, but she's fifty if she's a day. They say Mr. Anton is—"

Margaret interrupted gently before Poppy could expound on the obviously Balkan antecedents of Mr. Anton/Antonescu. "About the committee she wants me to be on, Poppy. It's for a . . ." She looked at the note Gloria Anton had handwritten on thick, creamy letter paper. "A designer showhouse. Is that one of those things where fancy interior decorators tart up a lot of rooms in an old house and the public pays substantially to gaze in wonder at the resulting excesses?"

"Exactly. For charity. A good one, one hopes."

"Gloria's charity is in aid of some organization that sponsors a disease," Margaret said. "Or perhaps it's the cure they're interested in. The SPDA. The truth is, Poppy, I don't have the time to do committee work. I'm taking edifying courses." On the table beside Margaret, Vasari's *Lives of the Artists* was open to the life of Giotto. She was thinking of getting back into the art-and-antiques business if her old employer, Bedros Kasparian, decided to reopen his shop.

"I've never set much store by self-improvement at your age."

"Poppy! My age?" Margaret might be rapidly drawing near to forty, but even so, she was many decades younger than Poppy.

"I learned everything I needed to know fifty years ago," Poppy said complacently. "Perhaps it was sixty. Please do try to help Gloria. I would myself, but it's a terrible world out there nowadays."

Poppy Dill often did not leave her apartment for years at a time, except for a few well-chosen social events of monumental importance, involving heads of state or selected megastars. It was known that both Jack Nicholson and Barbra were inexplicably fond of her, while Frank, who was her near contemporary, referred to her affectionately as "that wild old broad." There had been rumors of late about the state of her health, but as far as Margaret knew, she was as well today as she had been when they first met six years before, at the time of Margaret's arrival in New York from her native England.

"I don't think I can," Margaret said. "Really."

"It could be entertaining," Poppy said. When Margaret didn't answer, she added, "And terribly worthwhile." Then she made a final plea. "Gloria needs a reliable friend, Margaret. Her children are no support at all, and her so-called friends are often spiteful and cruel. That's why I suggested she invite you to be on the committee."

"You suggested! Poppy, this is so unlike you. Social matchmaking."

"I had to. She called and begged me to suggest a couple of nice women who weren't friendly with her ex-husband's current wife," Poppy said. "I assured her that you didn't know Angela Forsythe." Margaret agreed that, indeed, she did not know Angela. "So I told her you'd accept. The situation between the two women is, um, terribly hostile. Money, you know, and the problem of rejection." Poppy did not sound the least defensive about answering for Margaret about the committee, nor did she explain why Gloria, now remarried, felt such antipathy for her ex-husband's new spouse. It must have been a very unpleasant divorce indeed.

"I am busy studying Italian Renaissance art," Margaret said firmly, "and I am looking for work." Eminently presentable Margaret might be, but, alas, she was far from rich.

"But this will be perfect!" Poppy exclaimed. "One of the designers involved with the showhouse will certainly want to take you on as a consultant. Besides everything else, your taste is exquisite."

"The work I am seeking does not involve fetching and carrying needlepoint cushions and Victorian antimacassars for high-priced arbiters of taste and decor," Margaret said, but she had to admit to herself that the idea had a certain appeal. Choosing chintzes, selecting sideboards, evaluating epergnes . . .

"Seriously, Margaret," Poppy continued, "please do it as a favor to me." She paused, and when she spoke again, she sounded almost wistful. "Gloria's grandfather, the second Douglas Gilpin, was . . . well, he and I were rather involved . . . professionally . . . many years ago. I was just starting out in New York, and he was an important figure in social and financial circles. He was a widower, living alone with servants in his mansion on the East Side. I remember Gloria and her brother as children. Dougie ended up being quite successful. Douglas Gilpin the fourth. You must have bumped into him and Pauline. They're very social. Pauline's background is impeccable, just what Norma Gilpin, the mother, wanted for Dougie, but he almost ended up with . . . well, you don't care about his marriages. The other boy, Eric, died young years ago, before I knew the family. A tragedy that finished off Norma Gilpin, or what was left after the diet pills and booze had done their job. She had a wish to die, so there was the second tragedy poor Gloria had to deal with."

Margaret thought she heard Poppy sigh in a particularly pleading manner, as if attempting to bend Margaret's will to her own. It worked.

"All right," Margaret conceded wearily. She half resented being manipulated this way, but, after all, Poppy had been kind to her over the years. "I'll accept conditionally—out of respect for you. I'll go to the committee luncheon and see how much time it will cost me. But," she added warningly, "if Gloria Anton expects a daily dose of my attention to her showhouse, I simply can't comply. I'll let her put my name on the committee list."

"You *are* too good," Poppy said, and sounded genuinely grateful. "Now, you shouldn't mind Gloria's little ways. . . ."

Margaret felt a blip of alarm. " 'Little ways'?" she asked cautiously. A determined society woman of a certain age was one thing. A *mad* society woman was another.

"Gloria is a bit odd. Everyone will tell you that. She's prone to bouts of the vapors, I suppose you could say, although I don't hold with indulging in that kind of psychosomatic hysteria in order to have one's way. Certainly, she's always been known for her . . . firm opinions," Poppy said carefully. "When she was married to Leland, she did so much good charitable work, so she is used to . . . to having things done her way. I suppose being in charge of committees made her feel she was in control of her whole life. She simply dropped out of the business of doing good deeds when Leland ran off with Angela. A true scandal . . ."

"No, Poppy," Margaret said firmly, "I do not wish to hear the sordid details of anyone's marital history. I understand that your Gloria Anton is bossy, spoiled, and difficult, not very young, but likely very well clothed and coiffed, eager to regain her position on the social/charity circuit, now wed to a man who is probably younger and doubtless striking if not downright handsome, and someone certain people take pleasure in looking down their noses at. Is he in trade as well as burdened with a doubtful ancestry? Is he poorish, while Madame is well fixed financially?"

"Margaret, you must know her! You have her down exactly! Except that Peter is said to be quite well off, according to my sources, although certainly not as rich as Gloria, who inherited pots of money from Grandpa Douglas. Peter is in real estate and things. And he's actually quite a delightful man. I've known him for years. Women have always found him attractive."

Margaret thought there might be more, but Poppy had suddenly fallen silent. "I see," she said sweetly. "All right. I'll ring her and say I'll come to the committee luncheon."

"Thank you, Margaret. Thank you." Poppy was seldom effusive with her thanks. "How is De Vere? You haven't mentioned him."

"I haven't had the opportunity," Margaret said. She hesitated. Matters between her and Sam De Vere were delicate just now, and she didn't care to confide this to Poppy. "He's terribly busy. I think I soon won't have a honey who's with the police. He's considering retirement . . . pursuing a different career." If De Vere retired to the meadows of New Jersey where his parents lived, would he invite her along? And would she go— could she thrive so far from the bustle of New York City? Indeed, would he?

"Just as well," Poppy said. "I read every day about these terrible things that happen to policemen. But you don't sound happy about it." She waited, but Margaret refused to comment. "And dear Prince Paul?"

The affairs of Margaret's young friend Prince Paul Castrocani were easier to discuss. "He's convinced that he has found his princess," Margaret said. "Georgina, the girl he met in the Caribbean, Lord Farfaine's daughter. She's quite the heiress, which seems to suit Paul. They're due in New York shortly."

Paul, the son of the very rich Texan Carolyn Sue Hoopes and an impoverished Italian prince, was careening through his twenties seeking a suitably wealthy mate, much as his father had done successfully in the 1960s. Carolyn Sue was unwilling to continue subsidizing her son's jet-set lifestyle, although she owned the large apartment in the Chelsea section of New York that Paul shared, rent-free, with De Vere. Having very different modes of living, the two men had gotten on peacefully, but it seemed to Margaret that a ménage of Paul, the semispoiled Honorable Georgina, and De Vere would only serve to hasten De Vere's decision to move on to conquer new worlds.

Would that matter? she wondered. De Vere was seldom with her lately, and more than once she'd speculated that he had become involved with another woman. Margaret realized that except for her art-history courses and books, she was companionless a good deal of the day and night. Maybe it was time to get out and test the social waters again, and a stint on a charity committee was just the place to start. Maybe she and Gloria Anton would become fast friends, discussing the drawbacks of trompe l'oeil and the virtues of faux marbre as they worked on the showhouse.

Very soon after her conversation with Poppy, Margaret found herself speaking to Gloria Anton's maid or secretary, and saying yes, she'd join the showhouse committee for lunch two days hence at the Grandine, the exclusive private club in midtown Manhattan that harbored decorous old-money ladies.

"Madame will be pleased," said the maid. She had

an accent. Perhaps Peter Anton had taken on his mother or a sister so they could earn a few dollars. "I am placing your message just so. Madame will be seeing it when she is returning."

After hanging up, Margaret reread Gloria Anton's letter. She now detected in it a certain tone of Command Performance, and remembered Poppy's reference to Gloria's "little ways."

She noted down the date of the luncheon in her daybook. The opening of the showhouse was scheduled for May, nearly three months from now, when the sun would be shining and there would be no muddy footprints fouling the fine Scalamandre carpets. A very long way off, and plenty of time for flights of design fancy to be hatched. She turned to the volume of Vasari.

"It was a great miracle," she read, "that in so gross and incompetent an age Giotto could be inspired to such good purpose that by his work he completely restored the art of design, of which his contemporaries knew little or nothing. . . ."

Margaret looked up from her book to gaze at her East Side apartment. The twentieth floor provided a nice view of the city. The furnishings she'd chosen were comfortable, tasteful if a bit eclectic, but not lavish. Traditional-looking overstuffed, chintz-covered chairs and sofas, with some modern lamps, a few good antiques, some paintings from home. She wondered what Gloria Anton's interior-designer pets would make of her rooms. Would they find her taste ignorant and crass or simply uninspired? Certainly those trendy decorators would find Priam's Priory too fabulous for words. The family's Tudor estate in England wasn't exactly the height of patrician luxury, but it did have its requisite share of turrets, mullioned windows, a bit of armor, and some impressive antlers, and it was modestly decorated with *objets* collected over the centuries by traveling Priams, some of whom had had the wit to make off with valuable bits of other countries' national treasures at reduced prices.

Her brother David, the present earl, now and again mumbled about "returning" them, but as Margaret had pointed out, good Priam money had paid for them, and to whom exactly would he return the worn Oriental rugs, the slightly chipped (but authentically Greek) marble statue of Artemis, the timeworn Flemish and Italian portraits, and the admittedly smashing Gobelin tapestry?

Margaret closed her book and frowned. It really wasn't like Poppy to press one into committee work. She was a longtime witness to the follies of the New York upper classes, not a participant.

Margaret decided to telephone Candy Pierce, an acquaintance whose name frequently appeared on charity committee lists.

"Margaret dear, you can't mean you're going to accept?" Candy sounded appalled. "You've hit bottom if you're considering this thing that Gloria . . . What *is* her name now? I mean, her husband's a foreigner, sort of."

Ah, Margaret thought, and so am I, sort of.

Indeed, she was quite certain that Candy's forebears had been "foreigners" as well.

"Yes," Margaret said, "I've already accepted. It sounds like lovely fun, and Poppy Dill seems to think it's a good idea." Poppy still wielded power, not because of the things she revealed in her column but because of the things she pointedly chose not to print.

"Has Poppy been after you about this thing, too? I didn't know what to say to her, so I said maybe."

"Maybe you should say yes," Margaret advised, having decided she wasn't going to hit bottom alone. "It would be such a treat to work on something with you, Candy," she added without much sincerity. Candy did not seem to notice its absence.

"Well . . . I did feel terribly for Gloria when Leland dumped her for Angela, who has never been one of my favorite people, and has lately become completely impossible, acting far too grand for her station in life, if you know what I mean, but nobody's kept up with Gloria at all for several years, although Pauline Gilpin and Gloria are chummy. Gloria's . . . unstable. Always has been. I think it runs in the family. The brother drinks too much, and you must have heard about the mother's suicide, and God knows what other fine little messes that occur in everybody's family."

"You'd be perfect for the committee," Margaret said with as much unctuousness and enthusiasm as she could muster at one time, setting aside the question of Gloria's stability and refraining from noting that her own family attempted to stay clear of fine little messes. "So organized. And we could lunch. Often." Because of her title, Margaret always got the really good table in restaurants.

"I do have a lot of experience with charity things, although I've never done a showhouse. Gloria hasn't either, so we'll all sink or swim together. All right. I can fit it in, especially if I can get a few things at cost from the decorators for the new apartment Don is buying me. It's costing him a fortune, and so many rooms to fill."

Margaret cut her off politely. Huge New York apartments with huge price tags were not a preoccupation of hers. After hanging up, she called her truly dear friend, Dianne Stark, who, by virtue of marriage to the well-heeled Charles Stark, had risen rapidly from airline hostess to high-society hostess. It turned out that Poppy had been after her, too, to join the SPDA committee.

"What is going on with Poppy?" Margaret wondered aloud to Dianne. "She's pushing someone who doesn't seem to need pushing. Gloria was, after all, born a Gilpin."

Dianne chuckled. "The Gilpins . . . Charlie's family has known them, from way back, and he's told me all about them. Young Douglas—Dougie—travels in Charlie's business circles. You know, I think men are bigger gossips than a whole tableful of ladies-who-lunch. Charlie says old Douglas Gilpin should have ended up in prison, only the laws forty years ago weren't as tough on financial people as they are today. Dougie isn't much better than his grandfather. He's always skating on thin ice financially. Charlie says Dougie's always been furious that he didn't inherit as much from their grandfather as Gloria did."

"Apparently, Poppy had some sort of relationship with old Douglas. . . ." Margaret let her words trail off.

"Don't repeat this," Dianne said softly. "I mean, it's the only gossip I've ever heard about Poppy, and not all that many people know. Someone told me she blackmailed Douglas Gilpin into helping her get ahead in the newspaper world and society. She certainly had his backing, and no one could ever figure out exactly why. I don't think it was, you know, a sexual thing. It's too hard to imagine even the young Poppy entangled in a romantic affair with anybody, let alone the old man. I'm sure it was something else. Dougie was a wild young man, and there was the brother who died."

"Poppy mentioned a tragic accident involving a Gilpin boy," Margaret said.

"It happened ages ago. Gloria was still a teenager. Charlie got the story from young Dougie—well, he's not so young anymore. They were at prep school together, or maybe it was Yale. The younger brother fell and broke his neck at Douglas Gilpin's house, a terrible accident. The only reason it's remembered is because it's thought the mother committed suicide in her grief over his death. She was much beloved by social New York. Nothing blackmailable there. Poppy's seen and heard much worse in her time, I'm sure. First the accident, then the mother had a complete breakdown, and Gloria was hustled off to boarding school." Dianne paused. "I never thought of it before, but do you suppose Gloria was involved . . . ? You'd better ask Poppy."

"I definitely will," Margaret promised. "She must have tales about the Gilpins she hasn't told me. It seems their lives revolved around marriages, good ones and bad ones."

Dianne said, "Gloria's really okay, a little difficult and demanding. Spoiled. She sounds like everybody we know, doesn't she? She had a terrible divorce. . . ."

Dianne paused, and Margaret said, "See what I meant about marriages?"

"Everybody knows all about Gloria. When she found out that Leland was running around with Angela, they say she tried to kill them both. People haven't forgotten that. Well, she didn't kill them, and it's all right now. Charlie and I ran into her and her new husband out on the island last summer. Do you know what this SPDA thing is? Charlie wouldn't want me to get involved in anything that wasn't for—"

"A really good charity," Margaret finished for her. "It's printed in tiny, tiny letters on the bottom of the notepaper Gloria used. The Society for the Prevention of Dermatological Atrophy."

"Sounds perfectly awful," Dianne said.

"No," Margaret said, "simply inevitable. If I'm not mistaken, it's a society dedicated to the prevention of wrinkles. It's perfect, Dianne darling. The ideal charity for every aging debutante and her mother. For aging Gloria and for you and me."

"Don't be such a cynic," Dianne said. "It sounds like a very useful organization."

Chapter 2

Gloria Gilpin Forsythe Anton had spent the past thirty-seven years not walking along this particular street in the Sixties on New York's East Side. Once or twice, when she couldn't avoid it, she'd walked on the other side of the street, head down, so as not to look at the house.

Today she had to look.

"It's going to be fabulous," Bobby Henley called over his shoulder to her. "Fabulous! It's only one of those impossibly dreary millionaire's houses from the nineteen hundreds, but we're so lucky to get it on such short notice. It's going to be thrilling." He turned his baby-blue eyes on her and smiled. Bobby looked about nineteen, but he was in fact thirty, and an interior designer of considerable reputation. "And you will see that I get the room I want," he said. "Please, darling. Promise me."

"Strictly by lottery," Gloria murmured. "You'll have to work a trade with one of the other designers if you don't like the room you get."

She was only half listening. On the one hand, she was remembering the past, when her grandfather had owned the house, and on the other, she was willing her

15

designer showhouse to be a success: sixteen or so big rooms, a handful of small ones, plus three spacious landings and several large bathrooms to be decorated to death by two dozen of the best interior designers she could snag. The *Times* had promised coverage, and she'd already had a lot of interest from top decorators willing to invest in creating showcases for their work.

The proceeds from the admission fee to the house and from the pricey tickets to the private gala preview would go to the charity—and all the credit would go to her, Gloria, newly risen from the bitter ashes of her dreadful divorce from Leland Forsythe and renewed by marriage to dear Peter. A social diamond once again. Some of the luster, she was certain, would rub off on Peter, and that was all to the good. He needed people's respect to make his real-estate business a success.

Peter had helped her scour the city for a suitable house—big, empty, and preferably on the market. Then, to Gloria's surprise, he had suddenly announced that he and his partner had acquired this particular property, of all the houses in the city. An unoccupied town house he hoped to sell for many millions.

He must have known about her connection to the place—he had to, since she'd mentioned it often enough—but he never suggested that they live there. It didn't matter. She'd loaned him some of her money to keep his enterprises afloat, so, in a sense, she'd brought the house back into the family. Having the showhouse there would definitely improve its value on the market, because potential buyers invited to the private preview would see the spectacular possibilities of the place, and best of all, she had the house she needed without having to haggle through negotiations with a difficult owner. Peter was never difficult, bless him. What a difference from Leland's coldness and lack of sympathy for her problems. Peter had restored her to the warmth and affection she'd had from her grandfather and father.

Gloria pulled the collar of her mink to her chin against the late February chill and gazed at the Neo-Georgian facade of the five-story house. Decades of city grime had changed the original gray-brown stone to a sooty brownish black. The last owners hadn't bothered to clean it. The rows of tall windows were streaked and dusty, and she was shocked to notice that they appeared to be draped inside with yellowing bedsheets. She remembered the heavy red drapes in the second-floor library, and the dark mahogany paneling and the ceiling-high shelves filled with complete sets of leather-bound volumes.

Boris, Grandfather's butler, used to light a fire in the massive fireplace every day during winters. The table with the inlaid chessboard was always set with the intricate ivory and ebony chessmen trimmed in real gold and silver that Grandfather said were very, very old and very valuable. Her great-grandfather had picked them up somewhere on his travels. Her brother Eric had been the only one who liked the game. He played sometimes with Boris. Eric hated to lose, but Boris was a difficult opponent. Gloria imagined that all Russians were good at chess, because of all the chess grand masters.

People had called Eric "the quiet one," because he always seemed to be watching and thinking. Gloria used to think of him as a little Nazi, forever spying, and quick to tell Mother anything he fancied was damaging to his siblings. Mother wasn't always in a state to hear his tales, but she heard enough. Eric had been so different from her and Dougie, who was the oldest, and only liked cars and girls and riotous living up at Yale.

Dougie ... Douglas Gilpin IV. Every time she thought of him she felt a pain in her chest, like a steel band tightening around her heart. Thoughts of Eric made her feel the same way, especially today, facing the old house on a dreary winter's day.

A splatter of icy rain that dared to fall briefly on Gloria Anton's firm, gilded hair caused her to raise her eyes to the skies in annoyance. As if sensing her displeasure, the rain ceased. Meanwhile Bobby fidgeted at the foot of the steps, waiting for her.

Gloria stared at the house, and remembered one of the worst days of her life. It was the day before she was to leave, under protest, for the new boarding school in Connecticut.

She remembered the sound of sleet lashing against the library windows while Grandfather sat in his high-backed armchair, the newspapers on his lap, with Morgan lying at his feet. No, that was wrong. The old red Irish setter had died years before, and Grandfather had never replaced him.

It was the last time her life seemed whole, with Daddy and Mother, Eric, Dougie, and Gloria living together in their big apartment in the East Eighties, Grandfather here in his mansion with his servants Boris and Katya to mind him and the house, Miss Hannah to do his secretarial chores, and the fire always roaring.

"I'm freezing," Bobby announced. "Let's go in and look." He dangled the key to the front door. "Are you too appalled by it?"

"Certainly not," Gloria replied quickly. "A relative of mine actually lived here years ago. I'm just a little apprehensive about seeing what the place has become. I remember it as comfortable and quite lavish." She grinned wryly. "Definitely not a dreary millionaire's mansion. At least not to my childish eyes. I haven't set foot in the place in . . . years." She wasn't going to let Bobby know the exact number.

"I make formal apologies if I offended," Bobby said, "but I still think it's dreary." He took her arm and guided her up the four steps to the iron-gated door. As the two ascended, the tall blond woman, who no one would say immediately was a few years past fifty, and the youthful man looked very much like a youngish mother and her son.

Bobby turned the key in the lock with some difficulty and then pushed open the heavy door. He made a sweeping bow to allow Gloria to precede him. "Welcome to the future Designer Showhouse for the Prevention of . . . Darling, I can't remember the disease."

"It's more of a chronic condition," she murmured. "Not nice."

Bobby chuckled. "Whatever, the house is a sooty Cinderella today, but in just about three months— please God we can do it in that time—it will be transformed into a showplace for two glorious weeks. A mecca for beauty-starved citizens of the Tri-State area and a source of inspiration for all those poor souls who can't choose a carpet without help. Ugh!"

Chilly, stale air and dust assailed them as they

stepped into the foyer and then into the bare reception area. The walls were dirty, with nail holes where pictures had hung, leaving lighter rectangular areas on the grimy walls. Some light filtered through the cloth covering the windows that flanked the door and faced the street. Gloria was now certain that they were old bedsheets, stained and frayed along the hems. Could they be the same pristine white linen sheets that had once covered the grand high beds in the third-floor bedrooms in Grandfather's day?

Possibly. The house and its contents had been sold to a businessman not long after Grandfather's death, nearly forty years ago. The buyer himself was dead of a heart attack within a year, never having actually moved in. It then passed to a cultural/religious organization that had used it as an office for their Good Work, not as a residence. She'd heard from an acquaintance that they hadn't bothered to occupy the upper floors at all. The old linens could have been stored away in the attics all these years, along with the trunks and boxes of old clothes she remembered from childhood.

Bobby was almost dancing with pleasure along the long hall that led to the old dining room at the back of the house, pausing to peer into empty little rooms.

"Take a look at this staircase! The wood's still beautiful and it's remarkably graceful." He stopped and looked around with a judicious eye. "Not bad proportions, really, for a place designed by a hack."

"I believe," Gloria said, with the cutting tone she reserved for little people who were beginning to overstep their bounds, "that my great-grandfather hired the best architect of his day. . . ."

"Darling! Your great-grandfather built this? You never told me."

Gloria's expression eloquently said, "And why should I?" but her words were less haughty. "I never knew him. He was the first Douglas Gilpin, but my grandfather, Douglas the second, lived here when I was a child, and my father, the third Douglas, grew up here. My two brothers and I used to visit Grandfather often. He gave us wonderful lunches and let us roam around the place. My brother Dougie liked to hang about the billiard room in the basement, and Eric liked . . . well, he liked to know things. Grandfather—" She stopped and looked up at the dirt-streaked ceilings, cunningly decorated with ornate plaster garlands and swags. "He died here quite a long time ago." She stopped, and though the shudder that passed through her was faint, Bobby noticed it. "It's so . . . empty," she finished, and felt as though her soul had been stripped as bare as this house, her history erased, but not her memories.

"Gloria, are you all right? You're so pale. Please don't say you're upset to be in the house where your grandfather died," Bobby said, "just when things seem to be working out so divinely for the showhouse." Unlike everyone else in Manhattan society, he was apparently ignorant of the Eric affair.

"I'm not troubled at all," Gloria said, and willed herself to become both inwardly and outwardly calm. Bobby was a darling really, and a good friend, but she didn't need to share her troubles with him. "In any case, it looks so different. Now," she said briskly, "let's inventory the rooms and figure out exactly how many spaces we're talking about." The beautiful rooms of the showhouse, when complete, would give her back what she'd lost here to moving crates and time. "We absolutely have to get organized if we want to open in May, and my memory of the house is a little hazy."

But it wasn't. Not a bit. It was like being translated into the past by a time machine. Although the furnishings might be gone, she knew the exact details of every room, every stair and window and hall. She remembered the beautiful things that had filled the house: time-darkened family portraits, photos of the children in silver frames, and the signed, formally posed photos of famous men known to Grandfather, the little solid gold box she loved that was always on the mantelpiece, and, of course, the chess set. She could picture the heavy maroon drapes and the massive pieces of furniture in the drawing room and library that were perfect for games of hide-and-seek. She loved the sewing room upstairs, with its drawers full of old laces and ribbons, the steamer trunks in the box room, crammed with sparkling gowns for dress-up, boxes of feathered hats, and piles of ancient shoes.

She remembered the creaky old two-person elevator that ascended to the fifth floor, the big fireplaces, the enamel sinks in the kitchen, the old-fashioned bathtubs with lion's feet, the unexpectedly cozy little rooms where you could hide or nap or read a book from Grandfather's library, and the hidden backstairs that ran, narrow, steep, and dangerous, from the very top floor to the basement.

Most of all she remembered the last day she had been here.

She had long ago learned to force memories into a

dark little box deep in her head, but throughout the course of four decades, some managed to escape at odd moments to confuse and trouble her, and make her heart pound and stop her breath in the rush of an anxiety attack.

It had been sleeting that day, just as it was today. Mother had brought her around to say good-bye to Grandfather before she left for the new school. He'd promised her a farewell luncheon, with Katya cooking all her favorite dishes, although she was sure she wouldn't be able to eat a bite. The table would be set with the hand-embroidered linen cloth, the heavy old silver, and the prized heirloom china. Her brothers were to be in attendance—Dougie from Yale and Eric from his prep school. Mother, for once, hadn't suddenly remembered a more attractive lunch engagement, although Daddy would be absent, claiming to have Important Business at the Office. He had so much work these days; he was never home anymore to take Gloria to concerts or movies or to listen to her tales about school.

Mother had left her in the music room, to wait until Boris summoned her to Grandfather in his library. Dougie had looked in briefly then dashed off, to practice in the billiards room, he said, until luncheon was served. Then Eric had appeared in his beloved red-and-tan school baseball jacket, grinning mischievously.

"Grandfather hasn't come down to the library yet," he announced. "I was just there. Want to hear a joke? One last secret before you leave? It's really big, and it's going to fix Dougie for good." Eric and Dougie had always been rivals for the affection of Mother and

Grandfather. Gloria didn't care. She was everybody's favorite already.

"I don't like your jokes. It's all your fault I'm leaving!" she screamed at him. "Go away!"

She didn't want to hear any of Eric's jokes—which were usually wicked tattletale stories about someone, Dougie or her and her friends, or even Mother—especially not now, when her parents were ruining her whole life by having her hauled off to Miss Awful Person's School for Young Ladies somewhere in the middle of Connecticut, a state nobody went to unless they lived in Greenwich or Westport or went to Yale like Dougie.

"Poor Gloria," Eric crooned, but his eyes were bright with his malicious secret. "Jokes after lunch. Just you wait and see."

He left and closed the door to the music room behind him. She hated that knowing smile of his. Sometimes he could be so sweet and kind, and help her with her homework. Then, when he'd discover something secret, he'd change, begin plotting about who he could tell it to in order to cause the most trouble.

As she heard Eric's footsteps disappear down the hall, Gloria glared at the baby grand, which had never done a thing to her. She'd always liked the music room, though. There was even a harp, under a dusty velvet cover, that had belonged to her grandmother, who had died when Gloria was still a baby. Once Gloria had asked Grandfather if she could touch the strings, but he had firmly denied her request, the only time he'd refused her anything. The harp had not been touched since Grandmother's death, or so Gloria had been told.

While she had waited to be invited to Grandfather's library, she stood beside the harp and lifted the edge of the cover to reveal the gilded base, and the first strings. Cautiously she'd reached out a tentative hand and plucked once, twice. A silvery sound, like the breath of angels, surrounded her. It slithered across the room. . . .

Chapter 3

"*Your* grandfather will see you now."

Gloria froze guiltily at the sound of Boris's voice breaking through the liquid notes of the harp. The butler had a strong accent and equally strong anti-Bolshevik sentiments, having once had a high position in Czarist Russia. His escape from the new communist regime had brought him to the household of the eminently capitalistic Douglas Gilpin.

"Don't worry, Miss Gloria. It's not the sacred relic Mr. Gilpin makes it out to be. Miss Hannah plays it for him now and then, although she's certainly not as good as your grandmother was."

Gloria had frowned at that news. Hannah had never mentioned playing the harp for Grandfather, although she did occasionally play the piano for them. It seemed like a minor betrayal, but on that particular day, greater betrayals were still to come.

Boris left her alone in the library with Grandfather.

She was only fourteen, and she was scared about starting at the new school so late in the term. All the girls would already know each other. No one would want to be friends with her.

She was furious at having to go. She couldn't bear to leave. . . .

The grown-up Gloria halted her flow of recollections. She was trying to remember a face, the face of someone who hovered at the edge of her forty-year-old memories.

The man, René Crouzat, was the French teacher at her day school. Soft brown eyes, soft hands that had dared to stroke her blond curls. Soft lips that had brushed her cheek and awakened such a fire of desire. But that was all—nothing more, and never had she mentioned the shameful after-school encounters in his classroom, not to anyone, except once to Hannah, who swore she'd never tell. And once Gloria had written some words about him in her private diary, the one with the little lock.

Eric, in his lust to know everything, had crept into her room and read her secret, private words. Of course he'd known where she'd hidden the key. Then he'd rushed to tell Mother, who had to be restrained from storming the school to emasculate poor Monsieur Crouzat. She had ranted at Gloria as though she were utterly lost to all decency, and immediately arranged for her to be rushed away from New York to a school Gloria loathed long before she got there.

Once the immediate crisis over Monsieur Crouzat had passed, Gloria tried tears and tantrums about the boarding school, but these hadn't worked with her parents, even though she was the youngest child and the only girl and she had always had her way before. Her mother never again mentioned Monsieur Crouzat, but Eric continued to taunt Gloria with words from her diary until she wanted to strangle him.

It was Eric's fault that she had had to leave her pretty room at the apartment. She wanted to stay at home. She'd learn not to care when he taunted her. He was two years older and the smartest one in the family, everybody said so. She wouldn't even mind being teased by Dougie, who, at nineteen, was already a sophomore at Yale, but definitely not smart. Or so people said. She thought he was smarter than he seemed, since he did okay at school and he often came here to talk to Grandfather about business as though he understood it all.

That wasn't Gloria's concern. She liked Central Park down the street and across Fifth Avenue. She loved the shops on Madison Avenue, and Bloomingdale's, Macy's, and Gimbel's farther downtown, and even the Gimbel's at Eighty-second Street.

On that day when she was about to lose it all, she even thought fondly of her ugly day-school uniform. If she didn't have to go away, she'd promise never to look at dear Monsieur Crouzat again as long as she lived. She would take German instead of French.

Never mind. Grandfather would listen, understand, and obey. Her mother and father would obey him. Surely Eric had not dared to tell him of her passionate scribblings about Monsieur Crouzat.

Gloria patted her blond curls so they would look just so. She was wearing her black velvet coat with the white fur collar that she and Mother had bought at Peck & Peck. She looked like a little princess. That always worked with Grandfather.

"Grandfather, I don't want to go." Gloria stood before him, but he wouldn't meet her eyes. The single tear was wasted. "It's not fair. I want to stay right here in New York at my day school . . . please." She tried adding a quaver to her voice. "It's the best school in the whole world. Everybody says so."

However, Grandfather decided not to hear her.

"Sometimes we have to do things we don't like," he said. "The new school is excellent." He looked old and tired, as though he were wasting away to a shadow. "It's best that you go away. Make new friends." He paused. "Suitable ones."

She had a momentary panicky thought that Eric had told him about Monsieur Crouzat. Then he went on kindly, "There are plenty of holidays when you'll come home, and don't forget, Dougie won't be far away up there in New Haven. He'll visit. Besides"— he paused—"there are problems at home."

When Grandfather brought up problems at home, she knew she'd lost. Of course there were problems at home. Everybody she knew had problems. Her best friends, Karen and Molly, and everyone else had problems. In her case, Daddy and Mother fought daily behind their bedroom door when Daddy wasn't at the office or traveling on business. There were cold silences at the dinner table, and Mother's sudden bursts of irritation.

Of course, Mother had nothing to do except be irritated, shop, serve on committees, and take too many pills, which made her shrill and nervous and thin. She drank too many martinis at lunch with her friends, male and female. Eric had told Gloria all about that. He used to follow Mother around the city, sometimes even when he was supposed to be in school. After these lunches, Mother would come home and take long, long naps. Gloria remembered her shock when Eric told her that Mother had a boyfriend, although she refused to believe it at first.

Still, it had turned out to be true—Mr. Phillips, the husband of one of Mother's close friends. Eric wasn't often wrong. He'd even told her about the red-haired woman Daddy would take to dinner when Mother was out with her friends. Eric must have told Daddy about Mother and Mr. Phillips, because the fights and the suppressed icy anger at home grew worse. Gloria used to hide in her room, racked with terrible anxiety and barely able to breathe. Then came the trouble about Monsieur Crouzat, and the plans for boarding school.

"It's been difficult for you children," Grandfather said. "I wish your grandmother were still alive to . . . to advise about . . . things." He never referred directly to her parents' troubled marriage. "But you're a brave girl, like all the Gilpin women. I wish your father had married someone more like your grandmother. Maybe Dougie will. Lord knows, your mother is trying hard enough to set him up with the right kind of girl. You'll do fine at your new school. It's for the best, with Dougie in college, and Eric off in his own world." Grandfather frowned. "He's a funny lad, but he'll straighten out; at least he's got the brains. Dougie will be all right, too, if he behaves."

"I want to say good-bye to Hannah at least," Gloria said crossly. "Will she be at lunch?" Grandfather's young and pretty secretary was always nice to Gloria, showing her tricks about applying makeup—strictly forbidden by Mother—and taking Gloria on shopping expeditions when she wasn't busy with Grandfather's correspondence. Hannah knew all sorts of interesting people Mother wouldn't approve of if she'd known about them, artists and writers and musicians and people interested in political things. She could walk around Greenwich Village as though it were Park Avenue. Hannah understood the outrage Gloria felt about being forced to go to boarding school. She understood lots of things, about Monsieur Crouzat, whom she advised Gloria to wipe from her mind and avoid at all costs.

"Men will do that sort of thing, if they have the chance. Trust me," Hannah said. "And girls get crushes on teachers. But don't worry; just watch your step with him." She even offered to go to the school to speak to him, and maybe she did, because Monsieur Crouzat became distant and formal, almost hostile. Gloria loved him still, and her heart would beat hard if he laughed when one of the girls in French class made a silly mistake, and his eyes would crinkle in the way that made her breathless. But he never laughed for her now.

Grandfather said, "Didn't your mother tell you? Hannah's going off to be married. She's probably already left. I told her to be gone by today." He sounded angry. "She's not entirely honest and trustworthy, I conclude. Little things missing from the house, my household accounts a little lower than they should be. That's what girls are like nowadays. They'll do any kind of thing if they have the chance. No honor, no responsibility. And it's very inconvenient for me; I'll have to hire a new girl."

Like Gloria, Grandfather expected to have things his way.

Gloria was shocked. "Who is she marrying?" She ran over in her mind the young men to whom Hannah had introduced her. None of them, to Gloria's mind, was worth marrying, although some of them were really cute, and one or two had been quite sweet to Gloria. Still, it couldn't be any of them. Hannah said none of them had enough money to keep a woman happy.

Grandfather shrugged. "Some man," he said shortly. "One of these beatniks or commie foreigners from downtown. Probably doesn't have a penny to his name." Gloria didn't think Hannah would marry one of these men. "She could still be upstairs packing, but I've said all I care to say to her." He fumbled in the pocket of his vest. Grandfather always wore suits when he was in the city. He handed her a small red box. "Something to take to school with you. It belonged to your grandmother." Gloria hoped it was the gold box from the mantelpiece that she loved, but it wasn't.

Gloria had worn the ring on her little finger for nearly a year until someone at school stole it. Kathy Fields, she was sure, so she'd gotten even with her in subtle and cruel ways, even though she'd never liked the old-fashioned gold-and-garnet ring. It wasn't really *good* jewelry. Her father and her aunt Flora had inherited Grandmother's good jewelry. For all Gloria knew, Daddy still had his share stashed in a safety-deposit box. Certainly her mother had never worn it, or perhaps Daddy hadn't allowed her to. (Daddy's present wife was a sturdy, well-tanned tennis player who eschewed jewels. But they were promised to Gloria. Daddy had told her it was in his will, but Gloria was rich now, so she didn't much care about that old stuff.)

Gloria wondered if Grandfather was angry, not simply because he had to find a new secretary, but also because he would not have Hannah to play Grandmother's harp. But she didn't dare ask him.

"Gloria, come upstairs!" Bobby Henley's voice from the floor above echoed through the empty rooms and broke the chain of Gloria's memories. "I see it! I *must* have this room!"

Gloria ignored him and opened her leather notebook. Back to business. She wrote with a silver Tiffany pen in her beautiful clear hand, *First floor: the foyer, the reception room and hall, the dining room, three little rooms. Second floor: the library in the front, and the music room in the back, the long reception hall, the formal living room. Third floor: master bedroom in the front, Grandfather's dressing room and bath, three guest bedrooms and baths. Fourth floor: the landing, two nursery rooms in front, two servants' rooms, the sewing room and box room.*

She stopped. Not the fourth floor. Never, even if she had to disappoint some decorators. Gloria supposed she would have no choice but to go to the fourth floor and at least take a look. She was, after all, the chairwoman.

Hannah had redecorated the old fourth-floor nursery rooms for herself, using one as an office, while Boris and his wife, Katya, had occupied the other two, cramming them with gilded icons of Russian saints and pictures of the last czar and his family. The rooms always smelled faintly of beeswax candles and furniture polish, like a convent.

The attics on the fifth floor were not suitable for the showhouse, nor was the original old-fashioned kitchen in the basement and the musty billiards room next to it. The insurance people probably wouldn't allow the public to risk the narrow backstairs or the cramped elevator, even if it still functioned. She made another note to have the elevator inspected. She wasn't going to walk up and down constantly if she could avoid it.

"Gloria, darling . . ." Bobby, from above, sounded a touch impatient.

Perhaps they could use the fifth-floor attic space or, much as she disliked the idea, even the fourth floor, for showhouse offices, although that really was a climb, or they might settle themselves in the basement. If she had too many designers eager to participate, some of them might decorate the basement rooms, but the old kitchen was truly impossible. She'd see that the right kitchen designer was invited to do something fabulous on one of the upper floors, maybe those two girls whose work one saw everywhere. Perhaps the huge dining room on the ground floor could be divided into two rooms, with the kitchen at the back. The people who came to showhouses didn't care where the kitchen was placed as long as they could gawk at marvelous stainless-steel eight-burner ranges and rack upon rack of copper pots.

She closed the notebook slowly. Only then did she move gracefully toward the stairs.

When she reached the second floor, she found Bobby standing in the middle of Grandfather's library. The bookshelves, now empty, and the fireplace, with its elaborately carved mantelpiece, remained, but otherwise the room was stripped bare. Her footsteps echoed faintly as she entered.

"I *love* this room, darling! The proportions really are superb." Bobby put his hand to his brow as though experiencing a vision. "I see a gentleman's retreat, all leather and lush dark green fabrics, perhaps a touch of red, and all done up with the panache that has made me a legend."

"Be serious, Bobby," Gloria scolded. She stood at the threshold of the library, reluctant to enter.

After Grandfather had refused her pleas and given her the ring, she'd left him, and gone slowly up the main stairs to the third-floor landing in the hope of finding Hannah. Hannah understood it all—the day school, her fears about the new one, Monsieur Crouzat, everything. On the third-floor landing, just as she was about to ascend to Hannah's rooms on the fourth floor, she saw Eric creeping down the stairs. "Gloria, come upstairs," he whispered. "It's a real joke, better than I thought. Come and see."

She remembered starting up the stairs with Eric. She squeezed her eyes shut as if the darkness would bring Eric back, with his wicked grin, ready to tell her the joke she'd already refused to hear. She couldn't remember anything distinctly, except a sense of old anguish. Then, in her mind, she could see Eric standing at the door on the fourth floor that led to the backstairs. She could remember hearing a voice, seeing a person cross the hall from Hannah's rooms behind Eric. Then Eric was gone, and the person had disappeared into the hall leading to the box room.

She'd heard the loud thumping noise behind the wall between her on the landing and the servants' narrow backstairs, which allowed them to go about their business without being visible to the people of the house. Hannah's door was half-open, and just for a moment Gloria glimpsed someone standing there, still and quiet.

Gloria slammed the door to the stairs to block out the sound of Eric's fall. Then she stumbled down the main staircase to the third-floor landing, gasping for breath. She heard Katya scream far away, heard a commotion above and below, behind the wall, heard heavy footsteps. Boris was puffing up the main staircase from the second floor.

She heard the elevator descending.

She ran back upstairs ahead of Boris. No one was on the fourth-floor landing now. Hannah's rooms were empty except for the old desk in one room, a bed and a suitcase in the other, the last trace of Hannah. Boris and Katya's door was closed. A whiff of cigarette smoke hung in the air, and the faint scent of Hannah's perfume, Joy, the same perfume Gloria's mother wore, but she barely noticed as she flung open the door beside the elevator to reveal the backstairs, dimly lit by a single bulb on each landing. She heard voices from below, and Katya's plaintive wailing. In a panic, she started to scramble down the perilously steep stairs.

"Eric . . ." Her cry was scared and shrill.

"Stop!" It was Dougie's voice from at least two floors below, commanding and urgent.

She stopped, and blinked.

She was in the library, with Bobby Henley contemplating the carved wooden mantel of the fireplace. She wasn't little Gloria Gilpin now, but Gloria Anton, many years removed from that old tragedy.

"Of course," Bobby was saying thoughtfully, "I wouldn't mind awfully if I had to do the big room toward the back. What was it in your grandfather's day?"

"What?" Bobby's voice eased Gloria back into the present. The decorator's tendency to interrupt her thoughts could become irritating, she thought as she faced him, even though he was a dear, squiring her about when Peter was busy, and making her laugh with his biting gossip.

"The one halfway back? It was the drawing room," she said slowly. "The place where everyone gathered when something bad happened."

"Or something good, surely."

"I don't remember," she said. She took a deep breath. She did remember the room well. It was the place where they celebrated Christmas with the big tree, but Mother always felt unwell on family holidays, so they were never as festive as Gloria had anticipated. It was there they all gathered after Eric was found dead, his neck broken, lying at the foot of the backstairs. That's the scene Gloria remembered most vividly. Mother huddled in a chair sobbing, Dougie looking self-important, Boris and Katya disturbed and lost, Grandfather distressed but taking charge, sitting them down and patting Mother's head as though she were Morgan, the old Irish setter. Then Hannah arrived, dressed in a prim camel-hair coat and a perky hat with a red feather and proper gloves, come to fetch the last of her luggage but encountering death instead. Dougie took her aside and explained about Eric. Daddy rushed in later along with the doctor and a policeman. Everyone milled about the room, surrounded by noise, tears, and confusion.

Gloria closed her eyes and that scene vanished from her mind, but she now saw Eric again toppling over at the top of the backstairs. And then the *thump, thump* as he tumbled down behind the wall. The sound of the elevator. And the sense of a person standing quietly behind one of the doors. Someone breathing—or was it her own labored breath? She remembered thinking it was Eric, because she wanted the horror to end.

"We must get moving, Bobby," she said briskly. "Peter is meeting me for lunch, and getting a taxi today will be murder."

Murder. Someone—the policeman—had used the word that day, but only once, before Grandfather had given him a Look. The word quickly became and remained "accident." Gloria knew that what had happened to Eric was not an accident, but she never voiced her opinion. It might have been fate, or it might have been murder, but it was Eric's fault. His spying had finally caught up with him, and if he had accidentally tripped and fallen, it was probably because he was sneaking around, looking to find someone else's secrets to expose. She was left with only the knowledge that in the confusion, she'd sensed . . . someone.

"I really can't be late for Peter. He has so much to do."

"Your Peter's a lovely man," Bobby said unenthusiastically.

"Yes," Gloria said. "I'm so lucky to have found him."

After Eric's accident, her departure for boarding school had been delayed, but only for a week, for the funeral. The police asked her so many questions about what she had heard and seen. Her answer was invariably "Nothing," so they finally left her alone.

One nice policeman had taken her aside, though, and shown her a curious thing. In the palm of his rough hand was a chess piece from Grandfather's set—the beautiful, intricately carved black queen with a golden crown. "Your brother was clutching it in his hand when we found him," he said. "Know anything about it?"

"From the chess set," she said, breathing heavily. Had Eric stolen it from Grandfather? Unthinkable. "He . . . he liked to play chess. He played with Boris— that's the butler. He loved the chess set. He must have picked it up when he was in the library earlier." So that remained a mystery, too, and nothing beyond an accident was ever proved, and although Gloria carried her memories of the event with her through the years, she did nothing, suffering in the grip of anxiety attacks whenever memories returned.

Hannah had stayed on in New York for a few weeks, but not at the house. Grandfather wouldn't allow her to. Since Mother was prostrated by her grief over Eric's death, Hannah came to stay with them, and to take Gloria in hand. They'd attended Eric's funeral together, and Hannah had even gone with her to Lord & Taylor to buy a nice dark suit. She'd taken her to Greenwich Village for lunch "to take her mind off her sorrow," although Gloria's strongest emotion was guilt over the fact that she didn't feel especially sorry about Eric's death. They went to the theater, and talked about Life and Death. Monsieur Crouzat was mentioned once. Hannah said he was from a wealthy French-Canadian family and didn't really need to be a schoolteacher. Hannah was around the family so much it seemed that she couldn't leave them alone. She sat with Mother, she sat with Gloria. She even comforted Dougie, who shut himself in the den of the apartment and smoked and drank beer right from the can until he fled back to New Haven, away from all the grief. Hannah made amends with Grandfather for resigning, and found him another secretary, a chum of hers from the Village, who pleased Grandfather so much that she worked for him until he died, never living at the house, but coming in daily to open his mail and write his letters.

"Gloria, is something wrong?" Bobby's voice again cut into her private resurrection of the past.

"Nothing. Memories. I'd better get going to meet Peter," Gloria said, frowning. She was remembering the woman who'd replaced Hannah. Poppy Dill. She'd stuck to the Gilpins like flypaper over the years. Even with Grandfather gone, she was there all through Gloria's marriage to Leland Forsythe, through the trouble surrounding her divorce. Now, suddenly, she was being helpful about the showhouse.

After things settled down again, Hannah went to California. Gloria didn't even get to go to her wedding. Hannah never spoke about it or told her the man's name, but she knew. Poppy and Dougie had told her.

Hannah had married Gloria's own beloved Monsieur Crouzat. Later Dougie told her, gleefully, that they had divorced. She never asked him how he knew, but he and Hannah had been close after Eric's death, even going out in the evenings without Gloria.

After Eric's death, the family truly began to come apart. Dougie talked about quitting school and seeking his fortune out west. Then he was arrested up in Connecticut for drunken driving, but got off without punishment—Grandfather's doing, naturally. He stayed at home for a time, finished college, and went on to become the perfectly awful person he was today. Grandfather died several months after Eric, right there in his armchair. Dougie told her that Hannah had sent a nice note to express her sympathy, but couldn't come back from California for Grandfather's funeral. Gloria was glad. She never wanted to see Hannah again. Besides, Grandfather's death had made Gloria rich. He'd changed his will after Eric's death, so Gloria, to Dougie's distress, got their dead brother's share.

Over the next few years family get-togethers were tense and brief, with Dougie rarely coming home from New Haven. Mother withdrew completely from the social commitments that had meant so much to her, and died of an overdose of drugs and alcohol. They said it was accidental, but Gloria didn't believe it. Everybody said she had lost the will to live. Gloria grew still richer with the inheritance she received from her mother.

Daddy traveled farther away and longer, only barely managing to show up at Gloria's college graduation, and, shortly thereafter, to give her away at her wedding to Leland Forsythe, almost thirty years ago. Her analyst had convinced her that Leland was a father figure, that she had deliberately sought an emotionally detached man to marry. In any event, her father found himself a new wife with whom Gloria didn't get along, and they moved to Florida. He didn't bother to see his two Forsythe grandchildren until they were three or four years old.

Well, she never saw her children herself nowadays. Christine was too independent, and Eric—she had felt it was incumbent upon her to keep her brother's name alive—or Ricky, as she preferred to call him, devoted himself to bumming around the world at her expense. She thought he was presently in either India or Indonesia.

Gloria dropped her memories and said to Bobby, "Come along up to the third floor. Perhaps you'll find a room up there you like even better than this one. But don't worry, you'll have what your heart desires. I'll see to it that my committee assigns the rooms exactly as I wish. But we must hurry. I can't be late for Peter."

Chapter 4

*G*loria Anton brushed off the attentions of the
maître d' and found her husband at his preferred table
at Toujours Perdrix, the corner banquette, where he
could see who entered but could not be seen while
they were being seated in the narrow yet comfortable
restaurant. Understatedly fashionable, with an excellent chef who was actually French.

Peter looked up from his computer printout as she
sank onto the dark red leather beside him and allowed
him to kiss her cold cheek briefly.

"What a day!" she said breathlessly.

"What is the matter, sweet?" Peter asked. "You're
troubled."

"And you are too good about noticing things," Gloria
replied, glancing around. "Is anyone here?" Meaning, of
course, anyone worth noticing.

"Your brother. I told you not to mention Perdrix to
Dougie."

Gloria peered about the restaurant. "I don't see him."

"He came in, saw me, and headed straight to the
very back without speaking. He was with a woman
who is not Mrs. Dougie. I'm sorry, darling, but I can't
remember the latest wife's name."

43

"Nor can I," Gloria said. She and Dougie generally avoided each other, but she knew perfectly well that he'd been married for four years to Pauline Jansen, who'd once been married to Harry Jansen, whom Gloria herself had dated long ago during her college days. She got on well enough with Pauline, although she liked Dorothy, Dougie's first wife, better. Pauline and Dougie were far too chummy with Leland and Angela Forsythe. Dougie, of course, knew Leland from the time of Gloria's marriage. Mother, who had been a terrible snob, would have been pleased with Pauline, who came from a family that outshone even the Gilpins. Gloria had never managed to figure out why Pauline had chosen Dougie. She probably thought he had money, but Gloria's loans to him told a different story. "Who is Dougie with? Shall I find him?"

"Don't," Peter said promptly, to her relief. She wanted to tell him about the visit to Grandfather's house, and besides, she disliked her brother. "She's an older woman, very chic."

"I wonder who . . ." Gloria frowned deeply. Dougie had always been one for the ladies, but she thought Pauline had ended that.

Peter shrugged. "One of your society dames, I'd say."

A waiter poured from a bottle of pale wine into Gloria's glass.

"I shouldn't drink anything," she said. "I have so much to do. Peter darling, I must tell you about the house. . . ."

"I have at least two parties seriously interested in the place," Peter said, "and once they see what it looks like during the showhouse, they'll be clamoring to buy it. I see a bidding war—civilized certainly, but you know how these people are when they think someone else wants what they want."

"It was terrible being back," Gloria said, stubbornly refusing to hear him. "I didn't let on to Bobby Henley, since he'd talk. The last thing I want is someone remembering the trouble about Eric." She turned to her husband and gazed at his terribly attractive features, the thick brush of dark hair, strong eyebrows, and dark, sexy eyes. "But I don't know that I can handle it, Peter, being at the house every day for the next few months. I had a couple of very bad moments today."

"Henley is enough to give anyone a bad moment," Peter said. "But you don't have to be there every day. Eddie will stand in for you with contractors and electricians and all that."

"Eddie is a goon," she said shortly. She hated it when Peter was unkind about Bobby.

Peter laughed. "Yes, but he's *my* goon."

Gloria laughed, too, in spite of herself. Eddie Leone was Peter's all right, driving his car, handling matters involving his real-estate business, things Peter didn't care to handle, running interference, even fetching and carrying for Gloria, although she knew he didn't care for such chores, despite his accommodating and amiable way of carrying them out. He was also distinctly unpolished and dressed remarkably badly.

"I can just see him ordering two dozen interior decorators about," Gloria said. "They'll all be having hissy fits up and down the staircase."

"And all he'll say is, 'Yeah, yeah. Right. Now do it my way.' " Peter grinned. "And that's how they'll do it."

"I do love you," Gloria said suddenly.

Peter's expression seemed to say, Of course you do, but what he said aloud was, "The red snapper is recommended today."

Gloria wrinkled the perfect nose that her plastic surgeon had finally gotten right. "I thought a salad . . ."

"Darling, don't be tedious." He raised his hand to the hovering waiter. "The red snapper for both of us, then small salads of mixed greens."

"I don't want fish," Gloria said, evenly but firmly. "Steamed breast of chicken, no sauce. Peter, exactly who is interested in Grandfather's house?"

"You wouldn't know them," Peter said. "Not our sort."

She bit back a sharp comment about exactly what he thought "our" sort might be. Peter was sensitive about the differences in their backgrounds, even if he had, according to Poppy, once been married to a dreadful old French countess who had died.

He carefully folded the computer printout. "Go ahead, tell me about it, Glory. Was it really painful being back there?"

She relaxed. The conversation was now focused on her, where it belonged.

"It looks dreadful, naked and barren. No, you've seen it, you and Rich Centner probably know every nook and cranny, but you can't have any idea of the difference between now and the old days. I used to play in the music room, a lovely room. Now it's all battered walls and emptiness. Even Grandmother's harp is gone." She felt as empty as the house—without Eric.

"Want to hear a joke?" Eric had said, but he never

got the chance to tell it. There was no knowing what secret he'd uncovered, and whom he'd have shared it with. But as it turned out, the joke was finally on him. Gloria felt the knot of anxiety she'd lived with all these years, and tried to breathe deeply to dispel it, but she had to struggle to bring any air at all into her lungs.

"I can't talk about the house right now," she said to Peter as the waiter placed hot dishes before them.

"Are you having another attack?" Peter looked at her with concern, or his version of concern. "I do think it's good to come to terms finally with the old days. Your grandfather, the life you had that vanished with Eric's death, and your mother's. It drove you to Leland, and to trying to re-create the life you remembered. Such desperate measures never work, and it's been a mental and physical strain. . . ."

Gloria hated it when Peter turned into a pop psychologist. "Don't speak of Leland," she ordered. "It's bad enough that he puts his wife up to annoying me. I know it; you know it."

"I don't know it," Peter said. He tasted the snapper. "Delicious. Angela isn't annoying you."

The fork holding a tidbit of chicken breast paused at Gloria's lips. "Angela? You call her *Angela*?"

"No, darling, *you* call her Angela. I have never called her anything but Mrs. Forsythe. Don't do this."

"I'm sorry. I'm stressed. I keep imagining Angela will somehow spoil things. Somebody's going to tell her about the showhouse, the luncheon. . . . I mean, I asked Pauline to be on the committee, and she'll surely blab to Angela. Peter, at the house today, I kept remembering, seeing Eric fall—"

"Don't torment yourself, darling. You've told me a hundred times that you don't remember the details of that day. Being at the old house has made you remember things that never happened. We'll go back to the d'Este after lunch," Peter said gently, "and have a quiet, romantic afternoon." Gloria smiled at the idea of peaceful hours in the pied-à-terre they kept at the Villa d'Este hotel. Their principal residence was a lovely place on Long Island near the Hamptons, with sand dunes, seashore, and peace, far from the city with its anxiety-provoking memories.

"I have a hair appointment," she said, "and people to call about the committee luncheon."

"Cancel the hair, you look terrific. And two calls only."

Their eyes met. "All right," she conceded. She touched the fine English tweed of his jacket. "All right."

Angela, the second Mrs. Leland Forsythe, looked at the letter in her hand. It was an invitation from Gloria to Therese Thompson to become a member of her designer showhouse committee to raise funds for the distinguished charity SPDA. Terry had gleefully brought it to Angela, knowing, as everyone did, the animosity that raged between Leland's two wives.

"I'm too busy right now to do committee work," Terry told her, "although I wouldn't mind running a designer showhouse."

Her friend Angela Forsythe made an immediate decision. "I'll accept in your place. I might as well join this SPDA committee by the back door. Gloria will never ask me." She was mildly elated at the possibilities for future mischief. "Pauline will surely be asked."

Once she was there at the luncheons and committee meetings, she'd tell people that Terry had asked her to stand in for her, since Terry was going to stay at her house in the Caribbean to escape the Manhattan February. What could anyone do? Besides, Pauline was certain to be an ally.

Terry said, "Don't you go telling Gloria I had anything to do with your wicked plan. You're asking for trouble." But she was amused by Angela's ruse, and promised not to tip Gloria off.

"Gloria certainly can't cast me out without causing an unseemly rumpus," Angela said. "She won't want a lot of reminiscing about the divorce."

"Or her attempt to run you and Leland down on that quiet road in the Hamptons." Terry wasn't especially fond of Gloria, who in turn had little patience with Terry. "Besides, having you around for months—"

"Will serve her right," Angela finished, and smiled. She was convinced that Gloria was to blame for the fact that she wasn't welcome in the best circles in a manner befitting the wife of Leland Forsythe. "Everybody is always worrying about that damned 'poor Gloria.' They're all such transparent hypocrites. To hear Leland tell it, Gloria is hell on wheels, whining and complaining and taking to her bed with attacks of various kinds. Anyhow, I'm so much younger, even if I don't come from the same sort of upper-crust family as she."

She decided not to mention her little scheme to Leland just yet, but Gloria and Leland's daughter, Christine, was coming to dine that evening. She'd drop a hint about her plan and see how Christine reacted.

Dougie Gilpin's wife, Pauline, asked him whether she should accept the invitation to be on his sister's show-house committee.

"Whatever," Dougie said. As he approached sixty he was running to fat. "Don't you have enough to do?" Pauline could be a damned difficult woman. All the same, she was still pretty good-looking in spite of her age, she was always working out at the gym, she had a good brain, and she had stood by him, which was more than he could say about Dorothy, who'd bailed out at the first hint of a problem. He never should have told that one some of the dumb things he'd done as a kid. Pauline was more practical, unfazed by stories about his past indiscretions.

"No," Pauline said. She'd thought she was marrying Gilpin money rather than the man himself. As it turned out, there wasn't much money, and he was not an easy person to live with, but he was what she had, and she was determined to keep him. At her age, she didn't have much choice. "I like Gloria."

"I don't," Dougie snapped, and poured himself a hefty scotch. "And she doesn't like me."

Pauline sighed. "I know, but we do see Leland and Angela socially. I even go to the gym with Angela, and Gloria can't like that much, even with a new husband."

"Yeah, look at that guy Anton. My grandfather would have had him run out of town."

"Peter is sweet," Pauline said, unaware that sweet

Peter had trouble remembering her name. "And very good-looking."

"Scum," Dougie said. "And now he and his partner, that Richard Centner, have gotten their hands on Daddy's house, and they're trying to sell it for big bucks, probably have it split up into duplexes or something."

"Dougie, you were the one who put Peter onto the fact that the house was for sale in the first place. And I thought it was your grandfather's house, not your father's."

"Same difference," Dougie muttered as he topped off his drink. "It should have gone to Daddy when Grandfather died, and then it would have come to me when Daddy goes. But Grandfather changed his will, and the house got sold. At least Gloria didn't get it. But it's as good as hers now. Centner told me Pete got her to put in a lot of money so they could buy the place as an investment, since Gloria would never want to live in it. But it should have been Daddy's. And mine."

"Your father will live forever, so it would never have been yours," Pauline said. "Your stepmother is very strong-willed about such things. Probably something in those WASP genes."

One young woman, who possessed not only correct genes and impeccable ancestry but appealing good looks and an admirable intellect as well, burst into laughter when she opened the envelope containing a letter of invitation from Gloria Anton. The feisty but vertically challenged dachshund at her feet opened one eye.

"Listen to this, Angus," Christine Forsythe McDonald said to her husband. "My mother wants me to be on a *committee* for a charity!"

"Like the Red Cross?" Angus said, barely looking up from his computer.

"Hardly." Christine attempted to contain her mirth. "It's a decorator showhouse to raise funds for some society that wants to prevent wrinkles! Truly! Oh, Mother. I didn't think she even remembered our address. She must be desperate if she's pursuing me." She tapped a pencil against her head thoughtfully. "Still . . . if I accept, she'll probably feel she has to buy me suitable clothes to meet her friends, and I do need something fancy to wear to that conference banquet next month."

"It involves your great-grandfather's town house," Angus informed her.

"What?"

Angus swiveled his chair around to face his wife. "She told me when she rang you up. I forgot to tell you she called. She said she needed you."

"My mother has never needed me," Christine said, "except when I was young and was required for the family Christmas portrait of the happy Forsythe clan. The mummy, the daddy, and Christine and Ricky, the two adorable children. Or when she needed a cold compress."

"She sounded needy," Angus said seriously, but then, he was a serious young man. "You're between books, you're not teaching this semester, and I'll be off soon to London for research."

Christine wrinkled her nose. "I was thinking of going to Mexico," she said. "I've been wanting to have a look at El Tajín in Veracruz, and the murals at Bonampak, and then maybe go on to a dig in Belize."

"Think about it," Angus said. "It might do you good to get away from the bloody Maya and Aztec and Olmec."

"I've never been inside my great-grandfather's house," Christine said slowly, "although I've walked past it several times. Uncle Dougie always makes it sound like heaven, but he's not a happy man, so I guess he likes the memories. Mother's the same, in spite of what happened to Uncle Eric. She doesn't like to talk about that, but she's never let it go. Of course, you can't make that old cow Katya shut up about 'pretty, sweet little Eric, the sight of him dead almost in my arms.' I don't know why Mother keeps her on, she's a thousand years old."

"She's a damned fine cook," Angus said.

"What did Mother say she needed me for?"

"To go around to the house tomorrow morning."

"I won't do it," Christine said. "None of it. Angus, those society people. I couldn't possibly deal with them. I hated it all when I was a child, the party dresses and the dancing classes, and the teas with obnoxious old ladies, but now ... What would I talk about to them? Mayan glyphs? The Popul Vuh? Although," she added thoughtfully, "some of the bloodier activities of the pre-Columbians might appeal to them. Living hearts cut from the victims, bloodletting from the tongue and other body parts. No! I can't do it, not those thin women with the hair that refuses to move and the little suits that won't wrinkle." She giggled. "Even if their skin does."

"You deal with deans, academic colleagues, students,

scholars, Mexican officials, Mexican workers, tour guides at Mayan ruins, tourists following the tour guides, librarians, people on the Internet, editors, and me," Angus recited. "By comparison, your mother and her crowd are pretty straightforward."

"But I'd have to talk to Mother, and worse, follow her orders." Christine looked down at her shabby Reeboks and faded jeans. "Could you deal with a woman who owned a . . . a cocktail dress or two?"

"Sure," Angus replied cheerfully. "I could take you to dinner at . . . at . . ."

"Le Cirque? The Four Seasons? Only problem, love, is that you'd have to wear a suit. But"—she grinned—"maybe Mother will spring for that, too."

Angus said seriously, "You know you don't have to do any of the social stuff. You can stay behind the scenes, helping. She's never asked you for anything that I can remember."

"Except to pretend that I never see Daddy and Angela. We're having dinner with them tonight, remember. Well, if I can *do it* without actually *doing it*, maybe. But who was it who wisely said, 'Beware of enterprises requiring a new wardrobe'?"

"Lady Margaret!" The piercingly shrill voice on the telephone was like a steak knife to the brain. "It's Gloria Anton. How *are* you? How wonderful that you've agreed to be on my committee. How grand that we'll finally have a chance to meet!"

How does she manage to speak so fast and so much without an occasional breath? Margaret wondered.

And surely someone so apparently on the brink of hysteria should be sedated.

Gloria hadn't finished. "How much fun we're going to have, in spite of all the hard work it will require." At last she ceased; briefly. "Ah . . . Margaret . . ."

The tone had changed from false sincerity to wheedling. Margaret steeled herself for what was sure to be a request for a tiny but inconvenient favor.

"I have a little problem," Gloria continued. "Do you think you could spare me a few minutes tomorrow?"

It didn't sound too bad—yet. "Perhaps I could," Margaret said. "What is the problem?"

"Most of the decorators are dropping by the showhouse tomorrow, and I'd really appreciate it if you could be there with me. There's no one else I can ask. My daughter is terribly busy; she teaches and writes. I've asked my sister-in-law, but she's not sure. . . . Please. I need . . . someone. My husband is tied up. You know how men are."

"Yes," Margaret said, "I do." She knew that Sam De Vere often had pressing police business that caused Margaret to slip into second place in his life, but the urgency of dealing with robbery, rape, and murder understandably overrode any of Margaret's mild pursuits, which were probably only slightly more compelling than a designer showhouse was to a busy man like Peter Anton, with a wealthy wife competing for the world's attention.

Gloria had begun rattling off the address, the time, the plans for lunch. Margaret wasn't sure that she'd agreed to the favor, but apparently Gloria was certain she had.

"I can't do lunch," Margaret said. "I have an early-afternoon appointment." Or she would by tomorrow.

Then she mentally kicked herself for being vanquished by Gloria's "little ways." The woman had manipulated her into visiting the house, even if lunch could be avoided.

Well, how bad could it be?

Chapter 5

You've been persuaded to do something you'd rather not be doing, Margaret chided herself as she evaded the traffic on the avenues the next morning en route from her building to the Sixties and Gloria's showhouse-in-the-making. She was annoyed at herself for so readily betraying her solemn promise to attend only the committee luncheon and not to be at Gloria Anton's beck and call.

She paused on the corner of Third Avenue and Sixty-fifth Street and counted in awe the number of vehicles that appeared not to recognize the significance of a red light.

"Damned New Jersey drivers," muttered a bent, very tiny, and very old lady with a cane, an extravagant hat, and many scarves as she cautiously ventured a few steps onto the avenue, only to retreat hastily to the curb where Margaret stood.

"They can't all be from New Jersey," Margaret said.

"They are. You just look at those license plates. They probably don't have any traffic laws at all over there. Come along now, they've stopped, but the light's sure to change before I get across."

Margaret accompanied her, and in the middle of the

street, sure enough, the yellow "Don't Walk" sign on the opposite side began to flash. The traffic had the green light just as Margaret and her companion reached the far side, and the rows of cars, buses, and trucks surged forth.

Margaret parted from the woman, who was a familiar sight in the neighborhood. She headed in a downtown direction, and seemed to be walking briskly without leaning on her cane. No doubt it was a prop, to elicit sympathy or for fending off aggressive beggars. Margaret proceeded west, then north a couple of blocks, until she reached the Gilpin house. She mounted the steps, and because the door was ajar, she entered the foyer without ringing the bell. As Gloria had done the day before, she noticed the makeshift bedsheet curtains and the reminders on the wall of now-gone pictures.

The house was silent, so she called out, "Hello! Mrs. Anton?" The sound bounced off the empty walls with no response. Margaret decided to explore. Halfway up the staircase that Bobby Henley had so admired, she heard distant voices. Perhaps Gloria had found another patsy and Margaret could gracefully withdraw. She had a good deal of reading to get through before her art-history class that evening.

Suddenly a perfectly coiffed blond head appeared over the banister. "Lady Margaret? Thank you so much for coming. We're just looking over some of the rooms up here, so come along."

Margaret continued upward obediently.

When she reached the landing, she noticed a huddle of people surrounding the blond head—Gloria Anton obviously, since the head seemed to be in charge.

"Here's Lady Margaret Priam, everyone, a dear friend who's come to help us sort things out. Margaret, do you know everyone?"

Margaret glanced at the group—three men, three women, and Gloria—and saw faces she but vaguely recognized, yet they all nodded as though they knew her.

"Good!" Gloria chirped. "All friends here, but you can't have met Christine. This is my daughter, Christine Forsythe."

"McDonald," the handsome young woman said. "Mother cleverly ignores my married name. How nice to meet you, Lady Margaret." She seemed ill at ease, eyeing the others warily, as though they might be contagious.

Gloria said, "This is my sister-in-law, Pauline Gilpin, this is Bobby Henley, the very best decorator ever. At least that's what he says. He's everywhere these days, aren't you, Bobby?"

"I am, and it's a pleasure, Lady Margaret," Bobby said. "We met at old Kasparian's shop quite a while back, when I was trying to pick up a Ming knickknack or two for one of my clients."

"We might have done," Margaret said doubtfully. She hadn't worked for Kasparian for a number of years, and that reminded her that she really did need to find a job. East Side rents were rather high, and she did enjoy nice clothes and the occasional manicure.

"Never mind," Bobby said. "We'll become great friends in spite of our sordid collective past."

"Bobby, since you've seen the place before, why don't you lead Juana and Kenneth and the others through the rooms on this floor while I talk to Lady

Margaret." Gloria's tone made it clear that no arguments would be brooked.

Margaret saw the fair-haired young man with a cherub's face and a wicked grin elbow a slim, elegant dark-haired woman sharply in the ribs. She turned, glared at him, and stalked toward an open doorway leading into a darkened room. The others followed.

"Bobby, you are so naughty," Gloria said after him.

Bobby pranced back and muttered, "Gloria, why on earth did you invite Juana de los Angeles to participate in the showhouse? She loathes me, and I must say, I've never been terribly impressed by her work, or her title."

"Title?" Margaret asked, assuming he referred to the dark-haired woman. She knew just about every title in town, and this lady did not, to her knowledge, possess one.

"Purely honorary and limited to the world of decorators," Bobby explained. "We call her the Mistress of Mauve. I ought to catch up with them."

Gloria said firmly, "Let them amuse themselves looking at the rooms on their own. Bobby, you've already decided what you want, and Juana will probably claim the master bedroom on the third floor and turn it into a courtesan's boudoir."

"She certainly has a firsthand acquaintance with the requirements," Bobby said, turning to leave.

"Who are the others?" Margaret asked Gloria. "Bobby I've heard of, certainly."

He simpered, visibly. "Oh, Godfrey Helms is the one with the black hair. Dyed, of course. You must have heard of him. He does things on a grand scale, hotels and Brunei palaces, and the like," Bobby said.

"Lots of gold leaf and those monstrous patterned carpets. And he's never hesitated to steal an idea from his betters."

"He wants desperately to have a room in this showhouse, to show he's accessible to the ordinary person," Gloria said, "but I can't imagine what he'll come up with."

"I see chandeliers," Bobby said thoughtfully, "great huge dangling crystal chandeliers. Give him one of the little rooms, Gloria darling, so we can watch him pout and stamp his tiny feet in rage." He turned to Margaret with a glowing smile. "Godfrey also loathes me," he announced cheerfully. "They all do. It's jealousy, pure and simple. Oh, the other one here today in overalls is Kenneth What's-his-name. American Country look, all stencils and gingham, enough decorative bundles of twigs to build quite a bonfire. He's attractive, though, wouldn't you say, Lady Margaret?"

"Attractive enough," she agreed cautiously, not being certain of Bobby's criteria. She remembered the denim overalls, but nothing much about the rather large person wearing them.

"Where's Christine?" Gloria asked suddenly.

"She went off upstairs," Bobby said. "She seemed very keen on exploring the house. The ancestral home, she called it."

Margaret noticed the look of irritation that ruffled Gloria's features.

"She shouldn't be roaming about alone," Gloria said. "It could be dangerous. Until Eddie inspects the place, there's no telling what it's become."

"It's as solid as a rock, Gloria darling," Bobby said. "And didn't you tell me Christine goes exploring old ruins in the Mexican jungles as a profession? I hardly think an East Side New York town house poses any threat to an intrepid adventurer like her."

"It's just that . . ." Gloria headed for the stairs and bounded upward. "Chris!"

Good legs, Margaret noted, for a woman of fifty, as Bobby took her arm and guided her to the windows overlooking the street. He pulled aside the bedsheet to allow a little light to enter the room. "Gloria's been all nerves lately. The showhouse means so much to her, and very likely this house itself does, too. I hear"—he was almost whispering now, and Margaret was prepared to hear his version of the tragic accident that had occurred here—"that the house belongs in some sense to her husband and his partner, but a lot of her money was used to acquire it. Oh, yes, she inherited a pile from the grandfather and her mother and then there was the divorce settlement. Huge. So it's very much her house, past and present."

He stretched out his arms to take in the vast room in which they now stood. "I wonder why Anton didn't simply have the house done up right and then live here with Gloria. But Anton and Centner are fools who think they can sell the place for a fortune." He winked at Margaret. "Bet you that Gloria doesn't get a cent back. Still, it's a great address. Ivana's in the neighborhood and . . ." He shrugged. "People like that, if you like people like that."

"Well, her brother's death . . ." Margaret said, trailing off.

Bobby looked at her in bright-eyed surprise. "Dougie Gilpin is thriving, last I knew. I saw Pauline downstairs just now, and she didn't look the least bit

bereft. Of course, given Dougie's less admirable quali-
ties, perhaps that's not surprising. But"——he sighed——
"she was devoted to him. Go figure."

Margaret let him run on a bit, but she knew
she had to clear up the misunderstanding before *le
tout* New York started sending sympathy cards and
black-ribboned wreaths to mark Douglas IV's alleged passing.

"I meant the other brother," Margaret said. "The one
who died in a fall here in the house. Maybe that's why
Gloria is nervous about Christine."

Gloria reached the third-floor landing without hearing
an answering call from Christine. She continued on up
to the fourth floor, but not quite so quickly now. Slowing her progress was the memory of the last time she
had climbed these stairs, when all the bad things had
started happening.

To her left on the landing were the two rooms that
Hannah had occupied, to the right an alcove outside
Boris and Katya's room and the hall to the sewing and
box rooms, the small cagelike door to the elevator, and
the bland-looking door with the pale lavender glass
doorknob to the deadly backstairs.

It was dark up here, with only a wall sconce with
three tapered bulbs that gave off little light. Christine
must have turned it on.

Standing before the room Hannah had used as her
office, Gloria closed her eyes and took a deep breath to
still the rush of anxiety she felt building in her chest,
but the air up here seemed dead and unbreathable.

In the dark corners of her memory, she could see

Eric in his red-and-tan jacket at the open door to the backstairs, and an indistinct shape running from the office. "Here's the joke, Glory," Eric was saying gleefully. "Wait till I tell everybody. You first."

Gloria opened her eyes to see once again a person coming through the doorway.

Panicked, she started to scrabble down the main stairs, unsteady on her Charles Jourdain high heels.

"Mother!" Christine's voice followed Gloria down the stairs.

And then Gloria heard the groan of the elevator as it descended.

"I'll want every bit of wood in this room stripped down to the grain and refinished," Bobby was saying to an apparently attentive Margaret, who had happily developed the skill of appearing interested when in fact she was thinking of something entirely different—in this instance, Giotto's paintings of the life of Saint Francis, in the basilica at Assisi.

"There will be comfort to the ultimate degree, of course. A lovely thick, thick-pile carpet that oozes between your toes. And maybe a nice Sultanabad laid over it." Bobby put his hand to his chin and surveyed the room thoughtfully. "Do you think I could get away with a dog? As a permanent feature of the room, I mean. A lovely well-behaved black—no, chocolate—Labrador retriever, trained to loll luxuriously on its own little rug in front of the fireplace. Perhaps it should be a golden retriever, a bright platinum splash amidst the dark wood and fabrics." His eyes seemed to glaze over as the vision evolved in his mind.

"It would get terribly bored," Margaret said, "and someone would have to walk it from time to time. I doubt if the volunteer ladies would agree to that. And you'd probably need some kind of special insurance to protect you in the event of nipping incidents when the dog became impatient with the chattering Westchester and Long Island matrons."

"Then I'll hire a retriever wrangler to mind the dog," Bobby decided. "I'll dress him up in a gorgeous dressing gown. Lauren? Maybe. His look is about right for what I see for this room. I'll check on what Calvin has. The wrangler can sit here all day with his book and his dog and look simply fabulous. This city is full of actors looking for work, and it will knock the socks off the paying customers. I'll ask Gloria about the insurance question. She's got all these problem areas covered. Ah, here she is now!"

It was a sadly altered Gloria who almost staggered into the empty room that Bobby had been filling with his fantasies. Her golden coiffure was disordered, and her face drained of color.

"What's wrong?" Margaret asked, alarmed.

Gloria blinked, and seemed to be having difficulty breathing. "I . . . nothing. Something startled me upstairs."

"You should sit down," Margaret said, although there was nothing in the house to sit on. "The stairs perhaps."

"I'm all right," Gloria insisted. "Where's Christine?"

"Here I am, Mother." Christine appeared in the doorway. "What made you run away like that?"

"I heard . . . I heard Eric—I mean, the elevator. Was that you coming from the office?"

"I came out of a room I was looking at and saw you at the top of the stairs," Christine said. "Maybe it was an office. There's a big old wooden desk in there. It probably couldn't be removed without chopping it up, so they just left it. There was nothing in it except some old papers." She hesitated. "And this . . ." She thrust out her hand. Resting in the center of her palm was a black object shaped like a crenellated tower. The battlements appeared to be edged in gold. A chessman.

Gloria gasped at the sight, and started hyperventilating. She bit her lips and reached for the castle, but Christine would not give it to her.

"What's the matter?" Christine asked. "It's just an old chess piece. Very pretty, though. Made of ebony, I should think."

"And you came down to this floor in the elevator?" Gloria was agitated. "Oh, Chris, that was foolish. It hasn't been used or inspected in years." She was beginning to sound angry, although Margaret sensed that the anger was mostly a cover for her agitation. "And it is *not* 'just an old chess piece.' It's part of a very valuable set that belonged to my grandfather. You must never, never use the elevator."

Christine frowned. "Of course I didn't use the elevator, Mother. I walked down the stairs right after you."

"But I'm sure I heard . . ." Gloria looked puzzled. "Was anyone else up on the fourth floor with you?"

Christine's eyes flicked nervously toward her mother, then to Margaret, and to Bobby. The voices of the other decorators could be heard down the hallway as they returned to the library. "No. I mean, I don't think so. Once I thought I heard footsteps, but it must have been those other decorator people wandering about, or you coming up the stairs."

"How do you feel about dogs, Gloria?" Bobby interrupted. Margaret shook her head to stop him, but he ignored her. "A lovely golden retriever, say."

"We have dogs out on the island," Gloria said absently. "Peter seems to like them. My grandfather always had a dog here. I don't care much one way or the other. Why do you ask?" She was calmer now, and Christine looked relieved.

"It's a wonderful idea I had. We'll talk about it later. Come on in, Godfrey, Juana. What do you think of the place? Picked out your rooms?"

"I will decorate a bedroom," Juana de los Angeles said languidly, with a trace of an accent. "Lovely, lavish." She lowered her voice. "Mauve."

Bobby sighed heavily.

"I think," Godfrey Helms said after serious thought, "that I will beg for the large dining room on the ground floor. I had a vision of a long, polished table laid with heavy old silver and beautiful crystal wineglasses reflecting the light of—"

"A crystal chandelier," Bobby finished for him. "With black candles." He winked at Margaret. "You'll have to nail down the heavy old silver, my lad. The customers may be starved for domestic beauty, but they have sticky fingers. Where's Kenneth? Did our Country Boy get lost in the big-city house?"

"The dear boy met up with a caretaker person and they were talking structural issues. I can't imagine what Kenneth needs to talk about," Godfrey said. "I mean to say, all he has to do is paint the walls Williamsburg blue, throw on a border of stenciled flowers and birds, toss some patchwork pillows on a Shaker settee, and he has his patented look. Damned uncomfortable if you ask me."

"And me," Juana said. "I do so love the luxury of linen and lace, satin comforters stuffed with feathers. A canopied bed. Mirrors! Yes!" With this orgasmic affirmation, the señora closed her heavy-lidded eyes and seemed to remove herself mentally from their presence.

"I wonder who the caretaker is," Gloria said. "I authorized no one . . . Peter didn't mention . . ."

"Peter musta forgot he gave me the keys, told me to look the place over." A tall, heavy-featured man in a leather jacket, old jeans, and heavy work boots stood in the doorway to the library.

"Eddie!" Gloria said. "I didn't know you'd be here. Ladies, gentlemen, this is Eddie Leone, my husband's . . . assistant. He's going to be helping us with electrical things and the plumbing, the painting, any construction matters that come up, that sort of thing."

"Licensed? Union?" Bobby asked sharply.

Eddie Leone shoved his hands into his jacket pockets and scowled. "Yeah. You bet, buster." He did not appear to be impressed at finding himself in the presence of one of New York's finest young interior designers.

"Right." Bobby backed off quickly. The cold look that Eddie gave him warmed considerably at the sight of Margaret. She stepped forward with hand outstretched.

"Lady Margaret Priam," she said. "I know you're going to be a great help to us, and I look forward to working with you."

Eddie took her hand gingerly. He appeared to be instantly smitten, if the cowlike expression in his eyes was any indication.

"Eddie," Gloria said, and he managed to tear his eyes from Margaret, "were you riding in the elevator just a few moments ago?"

"You mean that little box I can barely squeeze into?" He laughed. "If you want to hear a joke, that's a joke."

Gloria put her hand to her breast and seemed to be breathing rapidly. "Joke? No, it is *not* a joke, Eddie. Someone was using the elevator; I heard it going down as I was coming down the stairs. I want to know who it was. Have I made myself clear?" She jerked her head around to look at the others. "And the rest of you. I won't tolerate . . . jokes." Her voice had grown shriller as she spoke, and spots of red that were not the result of the cosmetician's art appeared on her cheeks.

Bobby and Margaret hastened to her side, with Bobby murmuring soft words that Margaret didn't catch but that seemed to cause Gloria to relax.

As silence fell over the group Margaret was struck by the look of dismay that appeared on the face of Gloria's daughter.

Chapter 6

"I have to leave now," Gloria whispered to Margaret. "I have so much to do before the luncheon tomorrow, and there's the matter of the room assignments that has to be settled. Bobby has promised to stay here and show the house to the other decorators who'll be dropping by this afternoon for a look, and I suppose Eddie will hang around as Peter's eyes and ears. I don't know how I'm going to get through it all. I'm a wreck already." She looked at Margaret pleadingly.

Margaret said, "What would you like me to do, Gloria?" although it was obvious that Gloria would like nothing better than for Margaret to take her in hand. "Perhaps you and Christine or Pauline should go off quietly and have some lunch," but both seemed to have vanished. Eddie was still watching Margaret, slightly moonstruck, and the decorators were huddled together in a discussion, with the exception of Juana, who was gazing dreamily at the high ceiling.

"Godfrey, you ass." Bobby's voice was shrill. "Margaret, listen to this. He wants some great huge Irish wolfhound lying under his refectory table and that chandelier he's hanging over it. A dog!" Bobby was pouting prodigiously at the thought that someone had stolen his canine inspiration. "He'll probably want monks, too. And Gregorian chants."

Godfrey Helms brightened at this suggestion, and Gloria turned away from them with a sigh.

"Maybe you should simply go home and rest for a while," Margaret proposed. "Christine could go with you."

Gloria brushed back a straying hair and straightened her jacket. "Not Christine. We're creatures from different planets. She and those old Indians of hers are too bloodthirsty for me. Margaret, why would anyone want to torment me? I try to be a good person, even if I don't always succeed."

"Who is tormenting you?" Margaret wondered if this little hint of paranoia was another example of Gloria's "little ways," the celebrated instability which had been mentioned.

Before Gloria could explain, however, the room started to fill with people. A pair of nearly identical-looking, blue-jean-clad young women bounced in and rushed to Bobby, then Kenneth the Country Boy walked in with Christine and a man Margaret half recognized.

"It's Dougie," Gloria whispered. "That's all I need. . . ."

"Mother, look who I found in the basement. Uncle Dougie!" Christine said. "He and Kenny were playing pool. The old pool table is still there."

"Hello, Gloria," Douglas Gilpin IV said to his sister. "Reliving the old days?"

"I try not to," Gloria said. "Margaret, this is my brother, Douglas Gilpin. Dougie, Lady Margaret

Priam, who's helping me with the showhouse. Whatever are you doing here?"

"Pete said the house was open for your decorators,
and since Pauline was coming around, I thought I'd re-
live the past myself, show Pauline the place." Dougie
licked his lips nervously. "I've been meaning to call
you. This'll interest you. I ran into Hannah, the gal
who used to work for Grandfather."

Margaret noticed that Gloria's smile was fixed, and
that her eyes had turned hard. "What about her, and
why in the world would I be interested?"

"You know. She's in from the coast for a few days."
Dougie turned to Margaret. "She sure was a hot number in the old days. She's getting a bit long in the tooth
now, but still looks great. Hell, that was a good forty
years ago."

"I remember her only too well," Gloria said. She
seemed to be trying to control her temper. "I imagine
she's a bit old for you now."

That appeared to silence Dougie, but not Gloria.
"And Dougie, remember Grandfather's chessmen?
Christine found one today, in the office your 'hot
number' Hannah used to use. Was it she you were
lunching with yesterday?" She paused. "Ah, I suspected as much."

"We had some old business to discuss." Dougie
glared at Gloria, and then looked away, toward the
fourth floor. "You know, you're as bad as Eric, sis."

Gloria now spoke quite calmly. "Back to work. I
should introduce those two girls over there, Stacy and
Lacy, to Eddie. They're the kitchen designers. They'll
be needing his help with wiring and with putting in
cabinets. And then I really must leave." She headed

purposefully for the door just as a very grand gray-haired woman sailed into the room and forestalled her exit.

Dougie turned to Margaret. "I think we met someplace," he said. "Can't remember where or when. You one of my sister's bosom buddies?"

"Not really," Margaret replied. "She's asked me to help with the showhouse. I take it, though, that you're chums with her husband."

"Why do you think that?"

"You referred to him as Pete. Sounds rather chummy to me."

"Anton and I have had some dealings, outside the range of Gloria's meddling. You have to watch out for her; she's a devious one." He shrugged and grinned. "Runs in our family, I'd have to say."

"Uncle Dougie, I hate to interrupt, but . . ."

"It's okay, Christine honey, what's the problem?"

"No problem. Well, yes, there is. But . . . well, maybe Lady Margaret can help. It's Daddy. I mean it's Angela. She's fixed it so she's going to show up for Mother's committee luncheon tomorrow. Angus and I had dinner with them last night, and she flat out told me." Christine put her hands to her temples and grimaced. "It will make Mother nuts if Angela goes through with the idea. Why do I get put in the middle of things I don't want any part of? It's bad enough that I have to sneak around to see my own father."

"Will this turn out badly?" Margaret murmured. She directed her question at Dougie rather than Christine.

"Angela Forsythe," Dougie informed her, "is possibly even more devious than Gloria—my apologies for saying this about your mother," he added, looking at Christine.

The young woman didn't seem to mind. "Yes," she said to Margaret, "it will turn out badly, I'm afraid. Angela and Mother simply don't get along. I've never understood why exactly, since she's got Daddy, and Mother has Peter. . . ." She shuddered. "But of course, Mother got all that money from her grandfather. That never sat well with Angela or Daddy." She stopped talking as Gloria guided the imposing woman in their direction.

"Pete doesn't seem to mind," Dougie said. "He's reaping the benefits of the divorce settlement, and Gloria's inheritances."

"Shh, Uncle Dougie," Christine said.

"It's true," Dougie whispered. "I didn't get half what Gloria did from our grandfather."

"Mother says you didn't deserve to."

"What . . . ?" He looked alarmed but fell silent as Gloria approached.

"Lady Margaret," Gloria trilled. "You must meet one of today's *finest* decorators, a true legend in the field. Eloise Corbell. Madame Ambassador, may I present Lady Margaret Priam?"

"How do you do?" Margaret said, and searched her mental Rolodex for any Madame Ambassadors she might know. There was Mrs. Luce many years ago, and of course Pamela Harriman of late, but few others came immediately to mind. Margaret supposed that Madame had donated large sums to a successful presidential candidate and had been rewarded with an ambassadorial post. There was actually a slight resemblance between the woman beside Gloria and Barbara

Bush. Margaret suspected as well that the large double strand of pearls at Madame's throat was the genuine article.

Madame Ambassador nodded, as if reluctantly acknowledging Margaret's existence.

"And my brother, Douglas Gilpin, and my dear daughter Christine."

"I like this room," Madame said, ignoring the introductions. "I will make it a lady's retreat. I will have to lighten it up considerably. Pale blues, I think. Linen wall covering or silk. Yellow silk. A French feel to it. Yes."

Dougie looked around the bare library. "My grandfather had rather expensive tastes, but I don't think he would have condoned linen walls. Certainly not silk."

Madame raised an eyebrow and seemed to decide that Dougie did not rate even a look of contempt.

Gloria seemed unsettled. "Eloise, this room is promised to another decorator," she said hesitantly. One clearly did not cross Madame with impunity.

"Nonsense." Madame sniffed disdainfully. "There *are* no other decorators. Who?"

"Bobby Henley."

"My dear, that's a joke surely. I saw him downstairs. We'll settle this right now." She swanned away, with Gloria trailing her forlornly.

"Isn't she a fine old battleship," Dougie said.

"Ambassador to what?" Margaret asked.

"To one of the Scandinavian countries for a brief time," Christine said. "She was not appreciated. I don't believe the United States ever came closer to a war with Norway or Sweden or wherever it was than when Madame Ambassador was our envoy. You must remember the scandal about the lingonberries." She seemed positively cheered by the thought. "I'm going below to witness the fireworks. Imagine—Bobby and Madame facing off over this room!" She stopped at the door. "Uncle Dougie, I found the strangest thing upstairs . . . a beautiful old rook from a chess set. It upset Mother, I think, when I showed it to her."

"I imagine it would," Dougie said. "Do you have it? It belongs . . . belonged to Hannah."

"From what Mother's told me about this place, I should think it belonged to my great-grandfather," Christine said sternly. "Mother wanted it, but I didn't give it to her." She left abruptly.

"Douglas, who is this Hannah you keep mentioning?" Margaret asked.

"Someone from the old days. She was my grandfather's secretary. Good-looking woman. I was just a dumb college boy. It's funny the way things are working out. My kid brother found out some things he shouldn't have, and he was going to tell my grandfather, who was a bit sweet on Hannah himself. As a result, he overpaid her for the work she did, but Hannah always liked money. Eric should have been in the CIA. He was always sneaking around spying on people. Hannah hooked up with a guy who taught French at Gloria's school. Later she ran off with him and they got married, but it didn't last. She dumped old René Crouzat when he couldn't support her in the style to which she'd become accustomed here. Now she's finally come back, and got in touch with me. The thing is, Gloria had a big crush on Crouzat herself, like schoolgirls do. My brother found out about that and told me—and our mother, who couldn't get Gloria out of town fast enough. It was no big thing between them. I mean, Gloria was a kid, fourteen or fifteen. But he was French. . . ." Dougie shrugged. "Gloria never forgave Hannah. Or Eric."

"The brother who died."

"Yeah," Dougie said. "He had it coming."

When Dougie left her to roam about the old house in search of his wife, Margaret got out her cellular phone and called Poppy Dill.

"Poppy, I must know a few things if I'm going to stick with Gloria Anton's showhouse. The brother who died . . . was it really an accident, or was it something else?"

"Why would you think that?" Poppy asked sharply.

"Things people have been saying."

"You know how people will talk. It doesn't mean anything."

Poppy was being obstructive, but Margaret knew that even under torture, she'd never breathe a word she didn't wish to.

"You said you knew Gloria and her family when she was a child, and Douglas Gilpin. Did you know a woman called Hannah?"

"I knew a lot of people," Poppy said. "I still do."

"Don't be devious, Poppy," Margaret said, and remembered Dougie's use of the word. "Do you still know Hannah?"

"Hannah Garber was an old friend," Poppy said with what sounded like reluctance. "We met years ago when I was just back from poor war-torn Europe, where I met a lot of lovely people. The aristocracy.

Poor dears, they were so happy to have a nice American to entertain, although it wasn't like the old days. Ruins everywhere, and the food . . . my dear, you can't imagine—"

"Hannah," Margaret reminded her.

"Ah, yes. She helped me find two lovely rooms in the Village. She used to come around for chats."

"Did she confide anything to you about the Gilpin boy's death? Or about the man she ran off with and married?" When Poppy did not reply, Margaret continued. "She's back in New York. Do you know where I could find her?"

"Certainly not," Poppy said—too quickly. "Now, don't you worry about that old gossip. Concentrate on the showhouse."

"It appears that this showhouse thing won't be smooth sailing. One reason I called you is that the dreaded Angela Forsythe has gotten herself involved. She's planning on coming to the committee luncheon, uninvited and naturally completely unexpected."

"*Quel* disaster," Poppy said. "You'll have to do something about that right away."

"Me? I don't know the woman. I simply heard about it from Christine, Gloria's daughter. Apparently Christine sees her father and Angela from time to time, without her mother's knowledge."

"I should imagine she'd have to do it that way. Pauline Gilpin is a friend of Angela's; ask her to help. Or get Christine to help."

"I don't think Christine has much influence over her mother. And if she's been consorting with Angela, there could be a terrible family dustup. I really don't know Pauline."

"Please try." For the second time in a couple of days Poppy was pleading. Maybe her age actually was catching up with her. "I'll give you the Forsythes' address, and you could run around to her place and explain how . . . how unthinkable . . ."

Margaret was more inclined to seek out Hannah. Perhaps Dougie knew her whereabouts, but she tried again with Poppy. "Poppy, I said that Hannah is in New York. Where can I find her? Dougie's been in touch with her."

"Certainly Dougie would be, but never mind now about Hannah." Poppy began rattling off Leland Forsythe's address on Fifth Avenue and saying, "There's no time to lose. Gloria and Angela will kill each other if they come face-to-face."

"Look," Margaret said reasonably. "Angela is going to the luncheon, so if she plans to kill Gloria, she's made a very poor plan, and Gloria certainly wouldn't do anything unseemly to disrupt her event."

"You must stop it before it happens," Poppy insisted. "You have the address?"

"Yes," Margaret said. She'd scribbled it down, just in case. Then Eddie Leone sidled into the library and gazed longingly at Margaret as she spoke to Poppy.

"Can I do something for you?" Margaret asked him.

"You can get right over to Angela's place," Poppy snapped. It was not like her to be fazed by crises.

"I was speaking to someone else, Poppy," Margaret said. "I'll call you soon and tell you how matters turned out." Only then did she realize that she'd agreed to intercede between Gloria and Angela. She turned off the phone and slipped it into her bag. Eddie continued to look at her without speaking.

"Mr. Leone?"

"I was just . . . I wondered. See, I got to take Mrs. Anton over to the Villa d'Este, they got a place there, permanent, so's they don't have to drive back out to the island every time they come into the city. Could I drop you somewheres?"

Margaret hesitated. The Forsythe apartment was just over on Fifth Avenue, an easy walk. There was no point in letting Peter Anton's "eyes and ears" know what she was up to, since he could then easily share the news with Gloria. That would certainly only further complicate the showhouse situation, although admittedly, it would give Margaret a perfect excuse for escaping from the committee, or being expelled posthaste by Gloria.

"Thank you for the offer," Margaret said, "but I have an errand nearby, so I'll walk. I need the air after being in this dusty house."

Eddie's disappointment seemed to last only for a moment. "Quite a place, ain't it? I told the boss he should fix it up and live here himself, but no, him and Centner are planning on selling as soon as this showhouse thing is over."

"It's definitely Mr. Anton's property, then?"

"Yeah, him and Mr. Centner. You'd think the missus would want to live here, seeing as it was in her family years ago, but the boss said it's got bad memories for her." He shrugged. "Say, I could pick you up tomorrow if you're going to this lunch Mrs. Anton's having. Like at twelve? I got to drop her at the Grandine at eleven, so I'll be free." He looked at her hopefully, longingly. Margaret wondered how De Vere would react if he knew there was some competition for his lady love's heart. Maybe, she thought sadly, he wouldn't mind at all.

"That would be very nice, Mr. Leone," Margaret said, and gave him her address. "I'll be waiting for you downstairs in the lobby."

"All right! And say, you can call me Eddie." Eddie Leone was obviously transported to heaven, and a beatific smile brightened his heavy features. "You English? I mean, your accent and all."

"Yes. Yes, I am actually." Her accent became more pronounced. "And you can call me Lady Margaret. I think I'll just run upstairs for a moment. There's something I want to look at."

"Don't you go using the elevator. Mrs. Anton is right. It ain't real safe. I'm having a guy in to check it out. Okay, tomorrow at noon."

Moments later Margaret emerged from the library onto the second-floor landing. A slim, handsome dark-haired man was leaning over the banister listening to a tirade that emanated from below—Madame Ambassador giving her firm opinion to someone, probably the upstart Bobby Henley.

"Giovanni!" Margaret exclaimed. "Don't tell me you're involved in the showhouse."

Giovanni Millennia turned at the sound of her voice with a radiant smile. "Margaret darling!" He put a finger to his lips and whispered, "The most fascinating chewing-out is taking place below. Eloise Corbell is having one of her world-class fits, and that sweetie Bobby Henley is on the receiving end. But he did get in a couple of good body blows of his own."

"You designers take this business far too seriously," Margaret pronounced. She was growing tired of the entire interior-design world, and that without having seen a single innovative window treatment or any homage to Syrie Maugham.

"But it *is* serious. We spend a fortune doing up our rooms, it's really the only way we can advertise ourselves to the general public—the ones who aren't already fabulously rich and able to afford us without a second thought. But even the merely prosperous love to have their homes redecorated by classy guys like me. It's a big status thing for the upwardly mobile."

Giovanni was indeed a classy guy, Margaret thought, even though he was a homegrown Brooklyn boy who'd translated "John Miller" into his present, more exotic-sounding appellation.

"What are you doing here, Margaret?" he asked. "Going into the decorating business now that Kasparian has retired?"

"I'm on Gloria Anton's committee," she answered wearily. "It's turning out to be something of a chore."

"It's a hoot." Giovanni said. "We let our imaginations run wild, and if you are a student of human nature, you get to observe the depths of pettiness people can sink to. Need I tell you, it's a cutthroat business."

"I'm going upstairs to look at something," Margaret said, imagining a band of pirates swathed in Portault sheets and brandishing antique fire pokers awaiting her. "Care to come with me?"

"Don't mind if I do," Giovanni said. "I'd like to get an idea of what kind of room I might be handed."

Margaret looked surprised. "Don't you pick out the one you want and then proceed to fight to the death for it?" she asked.

He shrugged. "I can handle anything. I don't really

do kitchens, but I see that the General Electric Sisters are here, so no chance I'll have to worry about refrigerators and icemakers and top-of-the-line espresso machines—or even double stainless-steel sinks, for that matter." He followed Margaret toward the stairs leading to the next floor. "Godfrey Helms was babbling about monks and wolfhounds, and Kenneth will probably end up covering his floor with cow patties for the ever-more-authentic Country look he is seeking. I like nice English antiques myself, and my clients had damned well better like them, too."

Halfway up the stairs, Margaret asked over her shoulder, "Do you happen to know Angela Forsythe?"

"Do I ever! I actually did a room for her right after she married Leland. But only one. She's not as conservative as I am. Not that I'd ever let on to Gloria that I once worked for her. These women can hold a grudge forever."

"So you can probably tell me what happened to wreck Gloria's first marriage," Margaret said.

Giovanni was quick to reply. "Angela, pure and simple. It was the old story. Angie was an ambitious little secretary in Leland's office. She saw her chance, and she grabbed it. As you probably know, Gloria's always been kind of troubled. I guess things at home weren't easy for Leland, but she's been generous to a fault to me. And Angie's basically okay."

"Reasonable?"

"I wouldn't go that far. Why?"

"I have to talk her out of doing something she wants to do—badly."

Giovanni laughed. "Good luck. She's stubborn. Oh, but keep in mind that she's also socially ambitious, and terribly insecure. I'd say, if you can bribe her with the promise of entrée into the more rarefied strata of this social nonsense, she'd do your bidding in a second." He peered into one of the third-floor bedrooms and examined the ceiling and walls. "These rooms aren't bad. Probably bedrooms in the old days. I like bedrooms, lots of audio-video stuff, VCRs, hidden speakers, remote controls. A little bedside fridge, fat comforters, and pillows. But no mauve."

"You saw the Mistress of same, then?"

"Juana was sucking up to Madame Ambassador, who really does have an illustrious roster of clients. Movie stars, senators, the social climbers with nouveau money. All that refined WASP taste blows them away. Say, Margaret . . ." He was standing in the middle of an empty room, chin in hand, studying her. "I don't suppose you'd be interested in sharing your undoubtedly exquisite taste with the huddled masses yearning to breathe Chippendale?"

"In what manner?"

"You might consider signing on with me. I could use some help."

"A consultancy?" Margaret thought quickly. "I'd consider it seriously. I don't have enough to do. Right now, though, I want to go up one more flight."

Up they went, to a landing where the pale wall sconce was still lighted, and the door to the steep backstairs was ajar. Margaret peered through the grille on the elevator door. The car was two floors below, and she did not summon it up. Instead she went through the door beside the elevator—into the rooms, had she known it, that had belonged to Hannah in Gloria's youth. She noticed that two drawers of a substantial desk were slightly open and thought this was probably the desk Christine had spoken about.

Margaret's old nanny had a favorite proverb, which she'd never tired of repeating: "Nosy children lose their noses." Although Margaret had suffered childhood terrors about her nose suddenly dissolving or dropping off into a pudding, she had never overcome her tendency to look when there might be something to see. Approaching the desk, she opened one of the drawers wider and shuffled through the disarray of papers—a few paid bills addressed to Hannah Garber, an unsent birthday card, a chewed pencil, a white button. She tried the second drawer. The same sort of forgotten detritus of an old life. Margaret stopped to read a note from "Betsy," whose return address indicated she lived in Cleveland. Betsy Gallant. Betsy had big, florid handwriting, although she did not dot her *i*'s with little hearts.

Dearest Hannah,
Your news was so exciting! Congratulations, and Mom sends her love to you, too. Where will you live? We hope you'll think about coming home to Ohio, but I guess that's too much to expect. He has a lot to attend to for the next few years. I hope you'll come for a visit at least, so we can throw the two of you a big party. Please write me soon and tell me all the details.

Love, Betsy

Margaret pondered these words. Hannah must have announced her marriage to René Crouzat to the hometown folks. But wait. She seemed to recall that Hannah hadn't married Crouzat until after she'd left Douglas Gilpin's employ. The letter appeared to have been written before the marriage, or else it referred to some other exciting news, involving, however, "the two of you." Margaret put the letter from Betsy in her bag for future reference. Betsy did not sound like the kind of person who would leave Ohio, and maybe Margaret could contact her. She continued to search the drawers. Inside of one of the deep drawers, she found strips of masking tape, attached to the side, as though something had been taped there and removed.

She tried the long drawer in the center of the desk.

"Looking for anything in particular?" Giovanni asked.

"Just trying to get a feel for ancient history," Margaret said. "Only there's nothing here. Or nothing much." There was certainly no evidence that Poppy had ever occupied this space, but knowing Poppy, if she'd come upon the drawers full of remnants of the life of her old friend Hannah, she would certainly have looked at everything.

As she continued her surreptitious research Margaret's hand encountered a small, hard object wrapped in brown paper and tightly taped with masking tape. It went into her pocket without Giovanni noticing. She turned to him. "Madame's tirade must surely be finished, and I have to betake myself to the dragon's lair."

"*Ciao, bella,*" John Miller said, and sounded almost as Italian as Prince Paul Castrocani. "Angela's not really a dragon, just . . . ambitious. And please think about my offer. I could use a lady on my staff. A real one, I mean."

Chapter 7

*T*he brouhaha over the room selected by both Madame Ambassador and Bobby seemed to have been settled, and the decorators had vanished from the ground floor, along with Gloria and Christine. Margaret wondered whether Bobby or Madame had prevailed. She put her money on Bobby, who had charm, while Madame appeared to have merely a formidable bosom.

Margaret ducked into one of the small rooms off the ground-floor hallway and tore the paper from the packet she'd been clutching. The light wasn't good, but there was enough to make her gasp at the sight of the object in her hand. It was a pure-white horse's head, with a proudly arched neck and flaring nostrils, intricately carved from some hard substance. She contemplated the exquisite head, and memories of her years with Bedros Kasparian drifted back into her mind.

It was ivory, she decided, and the style seemed to be vaguely Oriental, like the fierce Han and Tang horses Kasparian used to display. It further appeared to be the knight from the same chess set as the black castle Christine had found, since the bridle was touched with gold.

Margaret put the piece away in a pocket, to study it later, since it was now time to slip away for her confrontation with Angela Forsythe. She worried briefly about simply shutting the front door without locking it. The appearance of Dougie easily solved this problem.

"I'm leaving now, and I seem to be almost the last one here," Margaret said, "unless Pauline is somewhere about. Giovanni Millennia is upstairs still."

"What the hell kind of name is that?" Dougie said sourly. "Pauline's gone off to her gym, as if daily workouts could halt the effects of gravity."

"It helps," Margaret said guiltily. She was not as attentive to exercise as she should be, partly because of the cost of health clubs. Giovanni's consultancy would help solve that problem. "Don't forget Giovanni."

"Where upstairs is he?"

"The fourth floor," Margaret said. "At least, that's where I left him."

"What were you doing there?"

She shrugged. "Looking around."

"It's not safe," Dougie said.

"Everybody keeps saying that. It looked safe to me."

"I don't like to go up there myself," Dougie admitted, and added, "It's where my brother fell. It used to give Gloria fits just talking about it."

"It seems it still does," Margaret told him. She hesitated, then said, "Gloria asked you about the chessmen. . . ."

Dougie looked at her sharply. "What about them? My grandfather had a fine set here, but someone was stealing the pieces. Probably old Boris, supplementing his income."

"You said the piece Christine found belonged to Hannah." Margaret thought for a moment. "Not Boris, but Hannah supplementing her income. Is that what Eric discovered?"

Dougie brushed the thought away abruptly. "More likely Grandfather was giving Hannah valuable trinkets to win her affection. Nobody much played chess here, except Eric. Funny thing, though. When the police got here that day he fell, they found the queen from the chess set clutched in Eric's hand."

"So maybe Hannah's little thefts—or gifts—really were what Eric had discovered and was going to report, and he was holding the evidence. But surely he wasn't going to tell your grandfather, if he was giving them to her. Did Hannah ever explain?"

Dougie shook his head. "There was no chance. I mean, she didn't say anything before that day, and afterward she . . . she wasn't welcome here anymore. I think she stopped in at the house right after the accident, but then I hardly ever laid eyes on her again."

"I see," Margaret said. She was fairly certain that he was lying. "Did you know or hear of someone called Betsy Gallant? An old friend of Hannah's?"

Dougie looked wary. "I might. How do you know her?"

"I don't. Her name happened to come up. Well, I must be off in a brave attempt to keep Angela from Gloria's luncheon. I suppose you can take charge of locking up—but don't lock Giovanni in."

"I'll see that everybody is out," Dougie said. "Eddie's

coming back later, and I'm still playing pool with that bumpkin."

"I don't think Kenneth is really a bumpkin," Margaret said. "Nobody is quite what they seem."

"Now that's the truth." Dougie paused, then seemed to have a sudden inspiration. "Say, you ought to come to dinner with Pauline and me sometime."

"I'm sure something can be arranged," Margaret said. "I say, would you know how I can get in touch with Hannah?"

"What do you want her for?"

"Oh, I don't. Gloria asked me to ask you about her," Margaret said quickly, crossing her fingers behind her back.

"That's a joke," Dougie scoffed, "after the trick Hannah pulled with that French guy Gloria liked so much. Well, it was one way out of her problems." Then he added slowly, "That's what my brother always used to say just when he was about to shoot off a bombshell. 'Want to hear a joke?' he'd say. Look, neither of you needs to see Hannah, and she doesn't want to see you."

"All right," Margaret said peaceably, although behind her smile she was calculating ways to locate the elusive Hannah.

"I hear you mix yourself up in all manner of murder and mayhem," Dougie said.

"Not mayhem," Margaret said, "not when I can avoid it. I really must run. Lots to do. You know." She opened the door and waved her best Royal Family wave, then shut the door.

In a matter of minutes she had arrived outside the imposing Fifth Avenue apartment building that housed

Leland and Angela Forsythe. Since she hadn't called ahead, there was a good chance Angela would not be at home, and thus she would be unable to do anything about dissuading her from attending the committee luncheon.

The doorman, uniformed to a degree that would have made him a fit participant in a Napoleonic war, eyed her suspiciously, but relented somewhat at the sound of her upper-class British accent. It always worked with doormen at swanky buildings. Anglophiles one and all.

"Mrs. Forsythe? She is usually out during the day, but let me ring the apartment. Lady Margaret, is it?"

Someone answered the ring, because Margaret heard the doorman speak her name in nearly reverential tones.

"Mrs. Forsythe will be pleased to see you," the doorman informed her. "The first elevator bank to the tenth floor. Left as you exit."

"Lovely," Margaret said. "Thank you so much."

The ornate elevator seemed terribly hot and close, but perhaps Margaret was simply suffering from nerves over the impending confrontation. As the elevator continued its stately progress upward she breathed deeply to relax, and thought about Gloria's peculiarities, which seemed to revive with the mention of her dead brother and the upper floors of her grandfather's house. Something was odd there, but Margaret resolutely ignored the quiet theme of an old murder running through it all. After all, it was not her concern. Her mission was to dig deep in order to find words to derail the apparently redoubtable Angela Forsythe.

The elevator shuddered to a stop and the gilded door

slid open. Margaret turned to the left and saw a woman standing in an open doorway. Not Angela surely. The plump, motherly woman with her graying hair in a bun must be a maid or housekeeper.

"Lady Margaret? Come this way," the woman said. "Mrs. Forsythe will be with you in a moment."

The apartment appeared to be vast, with huge arrangements of lilies and tulips and more exotic flowers scattered about the foyer and reflecting back from massive, ornate mirrors. The servant deposited Margaret in a sitting room filled with ponderous furniture—certainly not the English antiques beloved of Giovanni Millennia. The Persian rugs were good quality, and Margaret resisted the impulse to examine the painting of waterlilies, nicely lighted, on one wall. Monet didn't actually suit the room, even if the painting turned out to be an original.

"Hello . . . Lady Margaret?"

Margaret turned to face an attractively put-together woman of about her own age, wearing a nice heather-blue Chanel suit and chunky Chanel jewelry.

"I'm Angela Forsythe. I'm afraid I don't have much time to spare; you caught me just as I was about to leave. Please sit down, and tell me how I can help you."

Margaret sat. Angela was a cool one, all right.

"Perhaps I should start out by telling you that I'm a member of the SPDA designer showhouse committee," Margaret said. That seemed to take Angela aback, but only briefly. "And I must admit I'm a bit troubled about something."

Angela flushed and gripped her hands. "Terry doesn't mind at all," she said in a rush. "It's done all the time. You must know that. No harm."

"I must say I don't understand entirely," Margaret said, now confused. "Terry?"

"Terry Thompson. You must know her. A lovely woman. She's asked to be on just about every important committee."

Terry Thompson. Margaret recognized the name, and remembered the woman. An amusing acquaintance of Margaret's, not a friend really, but an enjoyable companion when circumstances demanded. She ran into her frequently at charity events, since it was true that she was an avid committee woman with excellent organizational skills. Margaret said, "I never imagined that Terry would be a party to . . ." To what? She watched Angela fidget nervously.

"She wasn't, I assure you. Well, not entirely. She simply doesn't have the time to be on the committee, so she asked me to go ahead and present myself in her place. It's the numbers that matter, not who the women are."

That wasn't strictly true, Margaret knew. An important name had its advantages.

"But it wasn't right," Margaret said. "Mrs. Anton has made very intricate plans—"

"Gloria." Angela spat out the name. "Who put her in charge anyhow?"

Margaret couldn't answer that, so she said, "I do think your reputation will suffer if you go ahead with this business. You know how people talk, and if you show up at the luncheon in . . . in Terry's place, you're going to be a . . . a joke among the people who matter. Surely you can see that."

Angela nodded, as though she agreed. Margaret

didn't dare believe that it was all happening as she wished so easily.

Her skepticism was well-founded.

"I intend to go," Angela uttered stonily, "and I don't care what you or Terry Thompson or anybody else thinks."

"I think you'd be doing yourself a good deal of damage socially," Margaret said. "You don't," she added somewhat cruelly, "have all that much clout."

Angela wilted a bit. "That damned Gloria can get away with murder—and I mean that literally—not to mention her attempts on my life, and I can't even be on a silly committee."

"It's not all that much fun," Margaret offered by way of consolation. "If you'd just reconsider, perhaps you and I could have lunch. I could see that you were invited to something when Princess Margaret or Fergie comes to town."

A shameless bribe, Margaret thought, and thank you, Giovanni, for the idea. Amazing what one will do to ensure a peaceful cup of chilled cream of broccoli soup and a nice piece of chicken. She had no illusions about the grandeur of the upcoming committee luncheon.

Angela, who had been looking terribly sad, as though a promised treat had been snatched from her hands, brightened as the significance of the bribe sank in.

"I owe it to Leland and our dignity," she admitted reluctantly, no doubt blinded by the imagined glare of tiaras, "but Gloria is so beastly to everyone. Not just to me, but to everyone—her brother and Pauline. She inherited money Dougie should have gotten, you know.

That's made it difficult for Pauline. I just wanted to get even with her."

"You may think of another, more effective way to achieve your ends," Margaret suggested benignly. "I have your word, then, that you'll not attend the lunch?"

"Yes." Angela sounded sullen, but then brightened. "When is Princess Margaret coming?"

"In the spring, I believe," Margaret lied. Thank goodness she hadn't promised a meeting with Princess Di or the Queen. "I'll be ringing you one day very soon to arrange our lunch, and then . . ." She shrugged. "So many lovely events to attend."

Angela walked Margaret to the door. "I'd love to have you meet Leland sometime," she said. "He's a dear. You can't imagine what he had to put up with when he was married to Gloria. She *is* a murderer, you know. She killed her brother. Leland knows all about that, she told him everything, and Leland got the rest from Dougie—how she pushed Eric down the stairs because he was going to tell her mother about her boyfriend, a teacher."

"She actually told Leland that?"

Angela tossed her head haughtily. "Everybody knows it. Leland thinks she's crazy. Well, she is. She even tried to run me down once out on the island. You must have seen she's very strange."

"I've noticed she's a bit . . . moody," Margaret said. "But we all have our difficult days."

"It's guilt that makes her totally nuts," Angela announced with conviction. "Someday it will catch up with her. Look, I have to hurry. I'm meeting Pauline at the gym, and then we're going shopping. Thank goodness I have friends like her and Terry, with an enemy like Gloria."

The two women parted, and it was with considerable relief that, a few minutes later, Margaret was able to return home and settle down with Vasari before she went to her evening class and met De Vere for a late dinner. At least he hadn't given her up completely. And she managed a call to Poppy to assure her that the Angela situation had been handled.

"I knew you'd do it." Poppy was thrilled. "What a wonder you are."

Margaret ignored this praise. "I hope," she said, "that you are keeping abreast of the exact dates of visits of the Royal Family to New York. There is a price to be paid for Angela's absence tomorrow. Now look, Poppy, I'm doing you a favor by helping Gloria. It's time for you to pay back by telling me about the Gilpins. The boy's death, this Hannah person, your relationship with Douglas Gilpin, and every other scrap of information you have about Gloria and her family. I mean it. I need to know about Angela and Pauline and Dougie—"

"Can you come 'round to see me?" Poppy interrupted. "I do dislike the telephone. They say that people can listen in."

"All right," Margaret said reluctantly. This whole business was already costing her more time than she wished. "I'll be there in half an hour."

The only thing to do now was to call directory assistance in Cleveland to try to track down Betsy Gallant. First she tried "Gallant, Elizabeth" and the street address on the envelope, but after forty years she wasn't hopeful about her prospects for success. There was, however, an Ernest Gallant at that address, and Margaret wrote down the number.

A weak old-womanish voice answered.

"Hullo? I'm trying to locate Betsy Gallant. I have her name from Hannah Garber."

There was silence. Then the voice said, "Poor Betsy's been gone since 1988. The cancer got her. Hannah, you say? I haven't heard that name for years and years. What's become of her?"

"She's visiting New York just now. I wanted to ask . . . is this Betsy's mother?"

"Yes, yes. Poor Betsy."

"Mrs. Gallant, do you remember hearing news from Hannah—oh, it must be nearly forty years ago, about . . ." About what?

"You mean about that rich boy she up and married? We never did get to meet him. Now, what was his name?"

"René Crouzat?" Margaret asked, though the term *rich boy* struck her as odd.

More silence. "I don't think so. I'd remember a name like that, foreign. It was something more American. She did it sudden like. You know what that means."

Then Mrs. Gallant had nothing more to impart. Margaret offered belated sympathy for her daughter's death and hung up.

It had turned colder since Margaret had left Angela Forsythe, and occasional snowflakes swirled down from the dull February sky as she set out for her visit with Poppy. Despite the weather, she decided to walk.

The doorman at Poppy's building recognized her and sent her up to Poppy's apartment, where the door had unwisely been left open.

"Poppy? It's Margaret," she called as she walked in.

"Come along to my room," Poppy responded from somewhere on the other side of the marble foyer. Poppy's room, Margaret remembered, featured a comfortable satin armchair that its owner referred to as her "interview" chair. Of course, the room also featured Poppy's huge bed, piles of pillows, and the old manual typewriter at which she pounded out her "Social Scene" column. No up-to-date computers for Poppy.

"Hurry," Poppy called out again. "I have a surprise!"

Margaret wondered if Princess Margaret had suddenly jetted in to lunch with Angela Forsythe. Probably not. Even the Concorde couldn't produce visiting royalty that quickly.

Poppy was on her bed, propped up on a pile of pillows, and swathed in her trademark gauzy peignoir. No princess was in immediate view, but Margaret saw someone sitting in the interview chair, half turned away from the door.

"Look who's here!" Poppy cried, but Margaret wasn't certain whether she was referring to her or to the woman in the chair, who appeared to be well into middle age, with short auburn hair and an expensive, tailored suit, with her handbag on the floor beside her feet, in their neat Gucci pumps. The woman stood as Margaret entered, but it was no one she'd ever seen before.

"I'm Hannah Garber," the woman said. "You must be Lady Margaret Priam, whom Poppy has been telling me about."

Margaret blinked. Good Lord, she thought. Poppy had conjured up the legendary Hannah.

"How nice to meet you," she said. "Your name has frequently been spoken today."

Hannah chuckled. "By the Gilpins, I suppose. Poppy said they were all swarming around old Douglas's house for some charity thing. You couldn't pay me enough to set foot in the place."

"And why is that?" Margaret was genuinely curious.

"I have bad memories of the house," Hannah said, "and I did some things I'm not proud of. Now, Poppy has lured me out of my hotel in this terrible weather because she said you needed to speak with me urgently."

Margaret raised an eyebrow at Poppy. "I did have an interest in seeing you," she admitted.

"It's about Eric Gilpin's murder." Poppy leaned forward eagerly from her cushion pile. "Margaret will figure it all out."

Hannah said gravely, "I'm not sure it wants figuring out, Poppy, and I certainly don't want to become involved with the family again in any way."

"You married Gloria's beau, did you?" Margaret asked.

Now Hannah laughed heartily. "I did marry. René was extraordinarily attractive, indeed irresistible. He was there for me when I needed him pretty desperately, but he wasn't really Gloria's boyfriend. He was twenty years older, and simply dallied—distantly— with her. It was harmless, but unforgivable, of course, for a teacher to do such a thing, although very mild in the light of today's goings-on between teachers and students."

"But when young Eric discovered the relationship,

and told his mother, she hustled Gloria off to boarding school," Margaret summarized.

"He was a vicious little boy," Hannah said. "He found out too many things for his own good. He even told his father about a harmless little flirtation his mother was having with a perfectly respectable gentleman."

"You use the word *harmless* quite freely. Did he find out something truly scandalous? So someone silenced him?"

Hannah said quickly, "The police determined he'd tripped accidentally at the top of the stairs."

Margaret was briefly tempted to bring up the chessmen that, according to Dougie, "belonged to Hannah," but instead said, "I suppose you remember Betsy Gallant from Cleveland."

Hannah sat up straight and lifted her chin defiantly. "I knew Betsy years ago. We have not kept in touch."

"Betsy died in 1988." Margaret noticed that Hannah relaxed a bit at this information. "Her mother is still alive. You must have shared your thoughts and secrets with Betsy, and she shared them with her mother. Your marriage and so forth. Eric's death . . ."

Hannah blinked nervously and looked over at Poppy, who was frowning. "Eric's death was an accident."

"But you told me what happened," Poppy said huffily. "And I believed it all these years."

"I know that after I set you up in the job with old Douglas, you blackmailed him with a farfetched tale about how Gloria had pushed Eric down those backstairs."

Poppy had the good grace to look uncomfortable. "But you said . . . And when Douglas took me on to replace you, and I brought it up, he was certainly convinced of its truth. But I never said it was Gloria. You said it was *Dougie*. I never told another soul, but naturally with Gloria being sent away to school so quickly, people started talking. Although," she said slowly, "don't I remember that the school affair had been arranged before Eric died?"

"It had," Hannah said. "She was sent away because of René Crouzat. Of course, Gloria was furious with Eric, but she wasn't alone in that. There were many things going on that he knew about, as Lady Margaret seems to have figured out." She smiled icily. "There still are. A lot of people were relieved when he died, but the repercussions of that time are still with us."

"Really?" Margaret asked, now reluctant to hear more.

Hannah smiled sweetly this time. "There was the mother, Norma. Did you ever suspect her, Poppy?" Poppy frowned, and Hannah laughed. "Don't worry. Norma doted on Eric, in spite of his tales." She sighed. "Well, she doted on Dougie, in a different way. The hope of the family." Then she stared steadily at Poppy. "There are some things even you don't know, Poppy, even now." Then to Margaret she said, "I didn't harm Eric, although Eric was well on the way to harming me."

"Because of Dougie?" Margaret asked. "The marriage and such?" Things were becoming clearer.

Hannah stood up suddenly and faced Poppy, who cowered against her pillows. "How dare you tell this woman!" Her voice was low and furious. "I told you something in confidence, so you would have leverage with Douglas, but you promised you'd never tell anyone else."

Poppy, pale but proud, said, "And I never did. Margaret is very clever."

"After all I've done for you . . ." Hannah let her words trail off as she stormed out of the room.

"And after all *I've* done for *her*," Poppy went on. "Take a look at those folders over there on the bureau. Clippings about the mother's death I didn't show you the other day. By her own hand. Very sad. She didn't bear up at all well after the boy died."

"You knew her, then—Gloria's mother?"

Poppy looked around, surprised. "Certainly. I was working for Douglas, remember. Norma would show up at the house, and sit upstairs by herself. All alone, because the old man put the fourth floor off-limits to everyone. Even Boris and Katya had to move to rooms downstairs. I went up there once or twice, but there was nothing much to see. I suppose she was thinking about Eric. And the family."

"And all the while you were blackmailing her father-in-law—his grandfather." Poppy looked momentarily taken aback at Margaret's word. "Everybody talks about it, Poppy, even you, so don't look so outraged. What I couldn't understand at first was how you dared to do it simply because of something Hannah hinted. You are certainly too smart to attempt blackmail without concrete proof that what you claimed was true. I imagine Douglas Gilpin the second would have needed to feel he was buying something more than just your silence."

"Well," Poppy said, "there was one document. . . . Let me tell you, I learned all about blackmail from an expert." She glanced at the doorway through which

Hannah had departed. "She showed me how it could be done—for a price."

"What document?"

"I don't think I can find it now," Poppy said reluctantly.

"So Douglas Gilpin gave in when you demanded—"

"Margaret, dear! I never *demanded* anything. I merely suggested that I could use a little help in return for his kind support, in exchange for which the information I had would never become public. I got absolutely *no* money. That would be dishonest. If Douglas chose to continue to send a little something to Hannah through me in exchange for *her* silence, that was his business."

"What information, Poppy?" Margaret demanded.

Poppy was silent for a moment. "They were young, foolish children," she said finally. "Dougie was much enamored of Hannah and they were . . . carrying on. The mother, Norma, was quite the social lioness, having married a Gilpin and all. She was eager for her children to achieve a similar lofty status. Gloria did all right for her—posthumously, I guess. The Forsythes are a very respectable family. It was Dougie, the fourth Douglas Gilpin, that she really pinned her hopes on. There were several very nice, very prominent young women she was hoping he'd fall for after he finished Yale and went into business with his father and grandfather. But he had a bad reputation at college, and the mothers of the girls didn't think he was quite . . . Still, Norma kept hoping, and then . . . Hannah was a very seductive woman in those days, and as she knew, Dougie had very substantial expectations from his grandfather. The perfect match."

"However do you know all this?" Margaret asked, and then added, as if to herself, "And why?" But she knew the answer. Poppy loved to know things. It was that simple.

"I got a lot of it from Hannah, who was a pretty close observer of the Gilpins. Hannah, presumably, got it from Dougie himself. I suppose that's what that little wretch Eric discovered, that his brother and his grandfather's secretary were having an affair. Hannah claims that old Douglas Gilpin himself had . . . well, made tentative advances. Nothing too strong or serious, but according to Hannah, he was quite taken with her." Poppy fluffed her hair. "Naturally I got some hints of that when I worked for him, but he wasn't the least bit attracted to me. I was far too businesslike. Anyhow, imagine what would have happened if Eric had reported the romance between Dougie and Hannah to his mother. Hannah would have been out of there, and Dougie would have been cut off from the family treasury. The grandfather never cared for him, and his relationship with Hannah would have provided a perfect excuse to cut him off. Norma would probably have felt the same way."

"Are you saying that Dougie pushed his brother down the stairs because he was caught snuggling up to Hannah Garber and he didn't want his grandfather to find out?" Margaret thought for a moment. "It doesn't work, Poppy. What else? The document you mentioned. They had gotten married, hadn't they? And then Hannah allegedly married René Crouzat to cover their tracks."

Poppy looked a bit flustered. "You seem to have figured it out," she said. And that was all she said.

Margaret took her leave, quite displeased with Poppy. She was sure there was more. Had Gloria known about her brother and Hannah? Had the mother?

She went home to prepare for her class and then to meet De Vere.

Chapter 8

"*I do* not want to become involved in dredging up an ancient murder," Margaret said. "I don't even know for certain if it was murder."

She slumped in the comfortable plush chair that was a special feature of the Country Wife, where she and De Vere were having dinner after her art-history class. She knew at once by the look on his face that she should have avoided the subject.

"I don't want you dredging up a murder either, old or new," De Vere said. In deference to the inclement winter weather, he wore a red cashmere turtleneck under his sport jacket, but his well-pressed jeans were apparently impervious to snow, rain, and sleet. "What murder?" he asked as he fiddled with the cutlery, rearranged the salt-and-pepper shakers. Margaret thought he must be gravely distracted, since he was normally not a fidgeter. She stopped herself from wondering if he was fidgeting because of her.

"Forty years or so ago," Margaret said, "a boy fell or was pushed down some steep stairs at his grandfather's East Side town house—a mansion really. It was reported in the newspaper as an accident. The family was quite prominent. I had Poppy show me the clippings, but the thing is, Poppy believed that a family member—his sister or brother—had done it. Eric—the boy who died—seems to have been an awful little spy, gathering information and sharing it with his elders. Anyhow, Poppy used information she believed to be true to blackmail the boy's grandfather, who in return helped her get a start in the news business and saw that she was introduced to a lot of socially and otherwise important people."

"A blackmailer? Not our Poppy!"

"Our Poppy," Margaret said sadly.

"So what was her proof? People don't usually give in to blackmail, unless the blackmailer has something more implicating than a strong belief."

Margaret filled him in on the history of Dougie and Hannah, concluding, "Poppy said she had a 'document' and that seemed to work with Douglas Gilpin. I believe it was proof that Dougie and Hannah Garber were married, since Douglas kept sending Hannah money, while Poppy got her start, met a lot of important people, and the rest, as they say, is history."

"But you have only her word that she blackmailed—"

"Poppy confessed," Margaret said, "but everybody knows the gossip." De Vere looked pained at the sound of the word. "In any case, the boy's death seems to have had certain repercussions, even if it was called an accident. His sister, Gloria Anton, as she is now, appears to have a hysterical fit when any reference to the death or the place where it occurred is made. The mother apparently committed suicide in her grief over her son's death." She thought a moment. "Or something else."

The pretty young waitress—the one who was "really

an actress"—hovered at De Vere's shoulder. "What will I eat tonight?" Margaret wondered rhetorically, willing the waitress to gain fifty pounds, catch a cold so her pert little nose would turn red, and have a bad hair day anytime Margaret and De Vere decided to eat here.

"Lamb chops, garlic mashed potatoes, and green beans," De Vere said promptly.

"That's what you'll eat," she said. "Meat loaf, broiled tomatoes, and a side order of macaroni and cheese for me." The waitress nodded and left, but not without casting a dazzling smile in De Vere's direction before her departure.

"So you only know what Poppy told you." De Vere was still watching the waitress. Margaret wondered if she was being paranoid about him lusting after other women.

"Not entirely. I've been catching hints of that old business. I'm working with Gloria on a designer show-house that she's running—in the grandfather's house, as it turns out. Her current husband bought the place— largely financed by Gloria, mind you—plans to sell it, but has made it available to her for this event. Petru Antonescu." Margaret shook her head. "I've met his sidekick, name of Eddie Leone. Not exactly your sophisticated man about town . . ." She grinned at De Vere. "He's got quite a crush on me."

De Vere looked at her thoughtfully. "Kind of a big guy? No neck to speak of?"

"And known to the police?"

"I didn't say that," De Vere said, "although I do know someone with that name. Not in a criminal sense, but you get a pretty good idea about who people are from the people they run with. Eddie fixes things, takes care of untidy bits of business. So he likes you, does he? Can I win back your heart by promising baked Alaska for dessert?" He signaled to the waitress and ordered the baked Alaska before Margaret could protest. It was all right, though. She loved baked Alaska, and she liked the idea that he thought he needed to win back her heart.

"Margaret," De Vere said cautiously. "You know I don't like you getting mixed up in this kind of matter. I mean it. And anyhow, if murder was suspected, even forty-some years ago, it wouldn't have been left hanging, with people still speculating." Now he was beginning to sound more like himself.

"You're right, of course. I wish I could get out of this committee thing." She told him about dissuading Angela Forsythe from attending the luncheon and about Madame Ambassador's tiff with Bobby Henley, although accounts of the goings-on of society people always made him impatient. "The potential for trouble is alarming. The decorators themselves are expert at backstabbing, Angela isn't going to let go without a fight, and Gloria is balancing on a very thin mental wire. If you ask me."

Then she proceeded to tell him about the curious matter of the chess pieces. "They might have been stolen from the grandfather, and they might be valuable. Just one more dicey thing Eric was involved in. I don't know how they all fit together."

"Why don't you consult with Kasparian about the chess pieces?" De Vere said as the enormous baked Alaska arrived. "He knows just about everything about anything of value. Thanks, sweetheart." The waitress beamed.

Sweetheart? Margaret stabbed a chunk of the brick-hard, meringue-covered dessert with her fork. That definitely didn't sound like De Vere, who was about as far as one could get from a wisecracking, sweet-talking television-series cop.

They talked then about Kasparian, whom De Vere admired a good deal. Kasparian had made his way by his wits, escaping from a war-torn homeland to reach these shores—where he had achieved a certain eminence in his field.

"Have you seen him lately?" Margaret asked.

"I was in his neck of the woods not too long ago," De Vere answered, "so I paid a call." The nice residential section of the Bronx where Kasparian lived wasn't exactly the woods, but as someone who lived and worked in Manhattan, De Vere tended to consider that borough to the north as, at the very least, a wild and uncivilized place.

After dinner, De Vere found Margaret a cab, and took off, he said, to meet his partner to pursue some police business. He didn't care to specify its nature to Margaret.

When she arrived at her apartment not too much later, it was with some relief that Margaret opened the door. The evening hadn't gone badly. De Vere had promised to call soon.

But why was the phone ringing, when all she wanted was to crawl into her warm bed and forget today?

Picking up the receiver, she heard a frightened voice say, "Margaret? It's me, Gloria."

Why was Margaret not surprised at her caller's identity? Why was Gloria gulping for breath? Another anxiety attack, brought on by what, this time?

"I know it's late. . . ." It wasn't, but Margaret didn't care to argue the point. "I didn't know who else to turn to."

"Yes?" Margaret queried with sinking heart.

"She's really back."

"Who?" Margaret had no idea what Gloria was talking about.

"Hannah. She married a man I knew years ago. . . . I had a silly teenage crush, but it was so real. He was so . . ."

"Ah, Monsieur Crouzat."

"You know him?" Gloria was surprised.

"Your brother was gossiping," was the best reply Margaret could come up with. She didn't mention that she'd met the woman in question, and that Poppy had been sharing her memories of working for Gloria's grandfather.

"My brother . . ." Gloria sounded vicious. "My former husband, my former friends . . . They're all out to get me."

Oh dear, Margaret thought, paranoia, on top of everything else.

"What about Hannah?" she asked. "Will you see her?"

"I've seen her," Gloria said. "We had dinner this evening. René's long gone. They were divorced years ago." Her chuckle was surprisingly bitter. "But she told me something else—not intentionally, I think, but it became clear to me what she was saying. I don't really like my brother Dougie, but I can't allow her to spoil the present because of some dumb things that happened so long ago."

"I think," Margaret offered, "that you dwell too much on the past, and expect that you can somehow change the present."

"People blame me for Eric's death." Gloria's voice had turned dreamy. Perhaps she'd popped a Valium or two and it was kicking in. "And then when Mother killed herself, they blamed me for that, too. I didn't like him, but I could never have pushed him down those stairs. Eric caused a lot of people trouble Mother, Dougie, Grandfather . . . There was someone behind that door."

"Behind what door?" Margaret asked politely.

"At the top of the house, in Hannah's office, where Eric fell. I went upstairs that day. I remember smelling cigarette smoke and just a whiff of perfume." She stopped, and there was a long silence on the line. "I saw someone—sensed someone rather—standing just out of sight as Eric was tumbling down the stairs. And then I left, but I heard the elevator going down. Ah, here's Peter." Briefly, Margaret heard Gloria speaking away from the phone. "I'm chatting with Lady Margaret, darling. I won't be a minute. Margaret, please don't say a word to anyone about any of this. And please don't be late for the luncheon tomorrow. I'm so afraid something will spoil it." If only she knew how close to spoilage the luncheon had come. At least Angela had been neutralized for the moment.

"I'll be there in good time," Margaret said soothingly. "Eddie Leone is driving me."

"Don't trust him," Gloria said, and lowered her voice. "He's Peter's spy. Bye."

Margaret heaved a sigh as finally, she was allowed to go to bed. Her last thought before sleep took her was to wonder if she ought to engage the Mistress of Mauve to add a few more touches of luxury to her bedroom.

Peter Anton sank into the chair that he'd especially ordered for their suite at the Villa d'Este. It was definitely not hotel issue, and Gloria had complained a bit about the cost, but Peter's partner Rich Centner had assured her that a superbly comfortable chair at day's end would make her adored husband better rested and thus more effective the next day. Gloria couldn't argue with that, so she'd paid, as she always did.

"Glory," he said, "we still have to talk about the fee for the use of my house for your showhouse."

"Fee? But it's *our* house." She was both alarmed and annoyed by his suggestion. "A lot of my money was used to acquire it—not that I like to think I own the place. I mean, I loaned the money to you for whatever purpose . . . but still, a fee?"

"It's just good business," Peter told her. "Richard agrees."

"Well, Richard isn't my husband, and you are, and I don't think charging your wife a fee for using a house whose purchase she largely made possible is good business at all." Gloria felt compelled to sulk. Pointedly. She could feel a headache coming on.

"Never mind that now," Peter said. "Did you have a good afternoon? I'm sorry I was too tied up to join you for dinner."

"I dined . . . with a friend." Gloria was purposely

vague. In reality, she had dined here with Hannah. Thank goodness Katya had left some food, prepared with her own arthritic hands.

"Where are you going?" Peter asked.

"I have a headache," Gloria said. "I'm going to bed. I don't know why I agreed to get mixed up with the showhouse. A fee, indeed."

Peter frowned. "We'll talk about it tomorrow. You don't look well. Is this house going to be too much for you to handle?"

At those words, Gloria smiled a strange half smile. "No, it won't be too much for me. In fact, it will probably do me a lot of good."

Peter Anton let himself out of their rooms at the Villa d'Este and rode the quiet elevator down to the lobby. Eddie Leone, looking frankly out of place among the potted palms, stood up as his employer emerged from the elevator.

"Mr. Centner is waiting in the town car," he said.

"Is the showhouse going to cost us a bundle in wiring and plumbing and reconstruction?" Peter asked.

Eddie shook his head. "Naw. The decorators get billed for the work they want done, except for stuff we got to do anyhow for code and the public's safety. The wiring's mostly okay, except the decorators want a lot of rewiring. I got to see a couple things are fixed up on the landings and stairs. The old elevator needs a look, but it's okay, too."

Satisfied with his answer, Peter got into the backseat of the black car and grunted a greeting at his partner, who was reading *The Wall Street Journal* by the light of a reading lamp behind his shoulder. Eddie moved the car slowly away from the curb in front of the hotel.

Centner looked up from the *Journal*. "Did you settle on the fee for the house?"

"Richard, I can't ask my wife to pay—"

"Pete, she's loaded, and besides, they can take it out of the showhouse proceeds. It's a legitimate expense."

Peter Anton didn't say anything for the moment, then he sighed. "I know we need cash. That estate we're going to look at over in Jersey . . ."

"It's a steal," Centner said, not for the first time, "and we can resell at a huge profit. Trust me. I know the business." He folded his newspaper and leaned back, smiling.

Peter looked grim. "I have other business to take care of first," he said.

Several blocks away, in the old Gilpin mansion, a single pale light was still burning in the ornate ceiling fixture in the big library on the second floor above the street. Bobby Henley sat on the floor of the empty room and gazed up at the ceiling. Dougie had earlier ordered everyone out, but of course, Bobby still had the key he'd used the day he and Gloria had first visited the site. He wanted to be there alone in the eerie silence of the empty house to imagine how he would create magnificence out of nothing in his chosen room.

At least he'd defeated that old cow Eloise Corbell in the war over who would get to decorate this room. Well, actually, it had been Gloria who had defeated Eloise. Bless her. And hadn't Eloise nearly foamed at the mouth when Gloria told her she'd have to take another room. There was no one who could carry off the persona of Autocratic Chairman better than Gloria, and not even Madame Ambassador could face her down.

As he looked around the bare room, he could envision the forms of the furniture taking shape, the heavy, rich draperies that would cascade gracefully to cover the windows, the beautiful golden retriever reclining on the rug in front of the fireplace. Now, that was a stroke of genius. His God-given talent was an amazing thing.

Bobby looked at the measurements he'd jotted down in his notebook. It would take some doing to get the room absolutely right, but he knew the firms from which he could borrow just the right pieces. They'd be listed in the journal and the suppliers liked the free publicity.

Getting up, Bobby turned off the overhead light and walked to the tall windows, his steps echoing in the silence. A car was illegally parked on the street and a pedestrian passed the house, walking a dog—a beagle, not the kind of dog Bobby had in mind at all. Light from a street lamp threw Bobby's shadow on the floor, elongated and slender.

These old houses are so peaceful, he thought, with his face to the light.

Then he heard the elevator ascending.

Half an hour later, as Bobby sat, huddled and motionless, in the darkest corner of the library, he realized he hadn't heard another sound since the elevator.

A defect in the mechanism had probably caused it to move without the intervention of a human hand on the button. Or Eddie Leone had come back to the house to check on it, and had now gone away. Maybe there was a caretaker about whom he knew nothing. But certainly there had been no footsteps, no sounds of doors opening and closing. Not a robber—there was literally nothing in the place to steal. Could it have been a homeless person who had discovered the front door open—surely it had been locked, Bobby told himself, but never mind that—and had decided to make the place his shelter for the night?

Let him sleep, Bobby thought, and was sure he could find his way quickly and quietly down the stairs to the main floor and depart without incident. But he wished his heart would stop thumping. He was not a brave person, and he had not brought his cellular phone today, with which he could have summoned assistance.

He yearned to leave. Archer was waiting at home at the apartment, and would not be pleased to see Bobby wandering in at all hours. He took a deep breath, and briefly sympathized with Gloria and her attacks of anxiety.

He shuffled across the floor to dim the sound of his footsteps and peered out onto the landing. Nothing to be seen, although it was rather darker than he had imagined it would be. The stairs were right at hand, and he carefully leaned on the banister as he made his way downward. Only a few more steps to the front door . . .

He unlatched the door to let himself out and immediately felt the chill of the February night on his hot face.

Then he heard the elevator descending.

Bobby fled, catching a downtown cab at the cor-

ner. It threaded its way recklessly among the cars on
the crowded avenue, but Bobby was less concerned
with the problem of New York City traffic than with
the identity of whoever it was who had been lurking
about the house. He didn't really trust Peter Anton, no
matter how dear Gloria doted on him, or his partner
Richard Centner, whose involvement in some real-
estate shenanigans had once brought him headlines in
the tabloids.

Bobby genuinely liked Gloria, and hoped that his
doubts about the strength of her relationship with Anton were misguided. She was a good friend, generous
and kind. He liked to escort her to the theater and to the
cocktail parties and dinners that Anton loathed. She'd
offered unflagging support a couple of years back during that terrible crisis when Archer had suddenly gone
off with a waiter.

Bobby shook his head. Things were all right now,
but one never knew when a monstrous twist of fate
would upset everything.

Chapter 9

Luncheon was to be served to the committee at one o'clock by the sturdy and amiable Irish waitresses of the Grandine Club, who labored long and hard under the critical eyes of New York's grandest dames. Their aprons were starched and their shoes were eminently sensible.

By noon, a pack of thin, lacquered, manicured ladies were already scattered about the main club room, at little tables or relaxing on sofas, clutching Bloody Marys or goblets of fairly decent white wine. Hermès scarves, Botteghe Veneta and Coach handbags, Ferragamo shoes, and Princess Borghese and Estée Lauder makeup provided a kind of theme to the gathering: expensive leather, expensive silk, and nothing too showy.

Margaret climbed the broad curved stairs from the ground floor and paused warily at the entrance to the club room, scanning the faces for Angela Forsythe.

"No sign of her," she said over her shoulder to Dianne Stark, whom she'd met at the door after being driven by Eddie Leone in Peter Anton's decently luxurious car to the very door of the stately building on Park Avenue. Dianne, given a hasty recounting of the

Angela bribe, agreed that there was nothing else that Margaret could have done.

"But there's Terry Thompson, after all," Dianne said. "She persists in thinking that Lucille Ball–red hair suits her."

"We all have our little beauty whims," Margaret said. "Mine, happily, have to do with largely unseen but very pricey undergarments. Where's Gloria? I see her daughter Christine. She's the handsome girl over there looking perfectly miserable."

"A very bright girl," Dianne murmured, eyeing the approach of a resplendent Terry Thompson. "And there's that old battle-ax Eloise Corbell. I didn't know she'd condescend to be on a committee."

"She's not. Gloria snagged her to do one of the rooms at the showhouse." Margaret turned to Dianne in horror. "Good grief, we're not going to have to deal with the decorators today as well as the committee ladies, are we?"

"It would seem so," Dianne said. "They're all here."

"A cocktail, madame?" The waitress looked as though the only acceptable answer would be yes, and Margaret, thinking of the committee ladies mixed up at close quarters with two dozen interior designers eager to impress them, had to agree.

"Yes," she said. "A Bloody Mary, please."

"Perrier," Dianne said. "Hello, Terry. I'd heard you'd gone off to the Caribbean."

"I had intended . . ." Terry began. "Then Angela phoned and . . ." She began to look flustered. "I mean, it's such a worthy cause, and I do love nice furniture and curtains, don't you?"

Margaret and Dianne looked at each other. What possible answer could there be to such a question?

"The decorators are such refined people," Terry went on. "That Mrs. Corbell is a genius, they say. Denise Markham had her whole house upstate done by her. It cost a fortune, but it's perfect."

To Margaret's relief, the waitress returned with their drinks and they were released from further conversation with Terry. Gloria was still among the missing.

"Christine . . ." Margaret caught her at the door. "Where's your mother?"

"She's downstairs in the dining room deep in conversation with Pauline, Uncle Dougie's wife. She's in a bit of a temper," Christine said. "She heard somehow that Angela would be here, but of course she's not. I called her and she said you'd—"

"Bribed her," Margaret said, and caught sight of Bobby Henley surrounded by a group of committee ladies. Then Kenneth the Country Boy, in brand-new jeans and a brilliant white shirt, drifted in, trailed by Juana de los Angeles and Godfrey Helms. Giovanni Millennia led a band of decorative ladies into the club room. They fanned out, greeting old friends and ordering preluncheon cocktails from the stolid waitresses.

A perfectly ordinary committee meeting, except that the chairman was absent.

And then she wasn't. Gloria Anton in a startlingly pink wool suit manifested herself at the center of the room and clapped her hands for silence, which was not, needless to say, forthcoming.

"Ladies, gentlemen . . . please . . ."

"She doesn't look at all well," Dianne whispered. There were, indeed, dark circles under Gloria's eyes, and she wore a slightly pained expression, as though she had a headache.

"We'll just go down to the dining room for luncheon and there'll be announcements and some assignments for a few of you. Our designers have drawn lots for their rooms . . ." She gave Bobby Henley a half smile. "We'll announce that, and then we'll get the SPDA Designer Showhouse under way."

After a scattering of applause, everyone began to file out and proceed down the stairs to the large dining room and its round tables, each set for ten. A long buffet table, laden with steaming hot trays and salads, occupied one end of the room,

"We'll be able to scoop up as many limp, lukewarm chicken breasts as we desire," Margaret said. "With a passable mushroom sauce, I don't doubt, and warmish rolls, cold asparagus, and a nice cup of soup, all in good friendship."

"They seem friendly now," Dianne said, "but they can turn on you so quickly."

Committee members and decorators were behaving like children eager to sit with their best friends, elbowing each other and tipping up chairs to "save a place" for a chum.

There was a tense moment when Bobby and Madame Ambassador seemed to be heading for the same table, but Bobby turned aside just in time, and found himself a place beside Gloria. Giovanni signaled to Margaret and Dianne, and they took chairs on either side of him. An unsmiling Pauline Gilpin sat next to Margaret.

Pauline said finally, "I had the most curious conversation with Gloria just now. She wasn't too coherent, talking nonsense about Dougie and his relationship with some woman years ago."

"Oh no!" Margaret's exclamation had nothing to do with Dougie and Hannah. It was caused by the sight of Angela Forsythe, who had just strolled in, head held high and apparently convinced that she belonged there in the suddenly silent dining room.

"So much for honor among the bribed," Margaret said to Dianne as she came close to choking on her cream of broccoli soup.

Angela graciously acknowledged greetings from friends while ignoring Gloria, who had stood up hastily at Angela's arrival, upsetting a water glass and dropping a spoon, a napkin, and the handbag from her lap. Bobby grabbed her hand and began speaking rapidly, perhaps urging her to reseat herself and let Angela pass. The committee ladies—all no doubt anticipating fireworks—leaned forward so as not to miss any fragment of speech that might pass between them. The decorators, perhaps less *au courant* on the history of the two women's marital affairs, were puzzled but deeply interested. Even Pauline leaned forward so as not to miss anything.

Angela smiled broadly, taking in everyone in the dining room, and proceeded slowly toward Gloria.

To Margaret's surprise and relief, Christine was suddenly at Angela's side, grasping her elbow firmly and talking into her ear as she attempted to guide her away from her destination. Gloria actually managed a faint smile and sank down in her chair. The waitress who had been standing guard at the buffet table was right nearby, busily mopping up the spilled water, while Bobby Henley patted Gloria's hand and spoke soothing words.

The object of all this concern, however, suddenly stood up, looking cool and calm.

"I'm sure we all want to welcome Angela Forsythe," she announced, "although I am sure she is aware that our little gathering is by invitation only. She must therefore be unaware of the traditional good manners to which the rest of us subscribe. Perhaps we can teach her by our good example."

Angela reddened, and in a moment she was gone, refusing to meet Margaret's eye as she departed. The tables continued to buzz with conversation, but the sensational moment had passed.

"Angela presses her luck, doesn't she?" Giovanni said. "Gloria, though, seems to have come through it well."

Gloria's blond head was close to Bobby's as they whispered furiously. Although her eyes seemed glazed from the shock of Angela's appearance, she otherwise appeared to be holding up well.

"I hate all this business," Margaret said. "Money and marriages."

"Except for the money part, I find it rather fun," Pauline said, "but I am glad there was no bloodshed, although . . ." She narrowed her eyes. "Gloria ought to know better than to interfere with my marriage. She'll go too far one day."

After the desserts were sampled and the coffee poured, Gloria again rose and tapped her water glass for attention. She made a gracious little speech about how successful the showhouse was going to be, briefly listed the various committees—the gala preview com-

mittee, volunteers, tickets, and the like—then sent
Christine around the room distributing floor plans with
each room marked with a big black number, and proceeded to announce which room had been assigned to
which decorator, the result of the random drawing.

Bobby Henley beamed when his number was announced. He had the library, as he wished. Juana de
los Angeles had the large bedroom on the third floor,
and it was agreed that the kitchen-designing girls
and Godfrey Helms would divide the big dining
room so that a kitchen could be installed behind it.
Giovanni nodded serenely at being assigned the old
music room.

Madame Ambassador received the drawing room,
while Kenneth would be working his Country magic
somewhere on the third floor. Someone named Alfred
Knox actually cheered when he learned he'd be doing
the ground-floor entrance hall. The landings were
handed out, and the bathrooms, the small reception
rooms on the ground floor, the remaining bedrooms.

"I will be the project coordinator," Gloria continued. "Lady Margaret Priam is second in command."
Margaret sighed and caught Dianne chuckling behind
her hand. "We'll be assisted by Mr. Eddie Leone . . .
who is unable to be with us today."

"My devoted admirer," Margaret murmured. "Insuf-
ficiently schooled in selecting the proper fork, and thus
unwelcome at the feast. He's probably glad of the re-
prieve." Dianne nodded uncertainly.

Gloria wasn't yet done. "If I or Lady Margaret is un-
available, my daughter Christine will stand in for us.
Our friend Terry Thompson has just today agreed to
postpone her trip to the Caribbean and take charge of

the journal, so you decorators will have to meet her deadlines. She'll be in touch with everyone. Dianne Stark will handle publicity, so report any good leads or potentially helpful contacts to her. We want the SPDA Designer Showhouse to be a resounding success."

Gloria was beginning to look exhausted, but pointed to a plump white-haired man who had raised his hand. "Andrew?" Andrew Collins had made a name for himself in Art Deco.

"What kind of access will we have to the house? What's the painting, sanding, papering schedule? The move-in schedule? Will you have guards? I have some rather valuable—"

"All in good time, Andrew. I'll be preparing the schedules this week and you'll have everything by next week. The house will be open to the decorators daily from tomorrow until the opening, although arrangements will have to be made in advance for weekends and holidays. The house will be secure, but I do urge you to have any valuables insured."

Dianne whispered to Margaret, "I remember one showhouse where robbers came in at night through the skylight and cleaned out the place."

Giovanni nodded. "And I remember the time when one woman came through with a huge shoulder bag and snagged a Lalique lamp. She was stopped at the door when she tried to carry out an eighteenth-century portrait in a huge gold frame. She claimed it was her ancestor, and therefore rightly belonged to her."

"They seem to like to take the flower arrangements," Dianne said. "The volunteers on guard don't brook that kind of nonsense, I can tell you."

"I wonder," Margaret said, "how Bobby and God-frey's dogs will fare."

"They'd better be housebroken," Dianne said.

Margaret stifled her chagrin at being named Gloria's second in command without prior warning or in-vitation, and by the end of the luncheon she had agreed to join her "leader" for tea one day soon at the Villa d'Este.

Giovanni captured her as she was leaving. "What-ever possessed Angela . . . ?" He sighed. "So you couldn't think of a substantial enough bribe, I take it."

"I did, and it was priceless. She betrayed me," Mar-garet said, now in reasonably good humor. At least she was to be spared the anxiety of having to corral a princess and a duchess into meeting someone they'd surely rather not meet.

"You must come to work with me." Giovanni squeezed her hand, then named a monthly retainer that caused her to shift her mental gears into fast forward.

"I could just manage it," she said, "but this show-house . . . is going to be a terrible bore."

"Not for me," Giovanni said. "I already have my room planned, and will start tomorrow. A couple of weeks to get the painting done and the furniture moved in, and then I can pick away at the details for the next couple of months. It's much easier when you don't have a client to deal with and it's all your own. Wait till you see how swiftly all these prima donnas get to work. You'll see. It'll be fun."

Chapter 10

*M*atters began to move along briskly as the early stages of the designer showhouse took shape, happily without Margaret's attentions. Gloria assumed a new and ever-more-commanding presence now that Angela Forsythe had been vanquished, and didn't seem to need Margaret's assistance for the moment, although she managed to call her almost daily to regale her with tales of spats among the decorators, problems faced and resolved, and to express her hopes for the success of the showhouse.

Since she had time free, Margaret decided to seek out Bedros Kasparian at his apartment in the Bronx and show him the knight from the chess set.

Kasparian, white-haired, distinguished looking, and as courtly as always, was effusive in his greeting. He examined the piece and frowned. "Ivory, certainly. Good quality. Quite Chinese in looks, but the Chinese did not play chess. However, the Indians did, as did Muslims from the subcontinent through to the Middle East. Very likely, it came from Mughal India, maybe to England by way of the East India Company. Then some affluent American robber baron carried it to these shores." He paused, then asked, "What are you up to?"

"It came into my possession," she said. "I was curious about its origins. It was part of a set owned by Douglas Gilpin the Second, but was discovered in a room of his mansion long abandoned by its occupant, who was apparently stealing the pieces. Valuable?"

"Valuable enough, if one had the entire set," Kasparian said. "This piece is lovely." He sighed. "I miss the shop, all my nice things."

"They're all gone?" Margaret was surprised. Kasparian's apartment, which was in a nice residential section of Riverdale, seemed to be filled with treasures, many of which Margaret remembered from the shop—the jade Kuan Yin, the beautiful celadon bowl, even the familiar red wall hanging made from a maharani's divali dress.

"I had to sell off some pieces to ensure a comfortable retirement," Kasparian said, "but I keep thinking about getting back into the business." He looked at her with a twinkle in his eyes under his white brows. "Want to go back to work?"

"I think I am back to work," she said. "Giovanni Millennia, the decorator, asked me to be on his staff."

"John's all right," Kasparian said. "Has a good eye."

"Do you know him well?"

"I've loaned him pieces from time to time, and he used to buy from me, although he wasn't a particular fan of Eastern art. You say this piece belonged to Douglas Gilpin? He was quite a piece of work. I knew him right after the war, from which, I believe, he profited mightily. I seem to remember some sort of trouble involving him back in the fifties."

."The death of his grandson at his house." She explained her connection with the Gilpins and he listened closely, nodding from time to time. "The house is now owned by Peter Anton, the current husband of Gloria Gilpin."

"It doesn't pay to get mixed up with people like Anton," Kasparian warned. "He is—" He stopped. "I don't care to gossip."

"You can't leave me hanging like that," Margaret said. "He's what?"

"I'd call him shady. I used to run into him in Paris from time to time a dozen or twenty years ago. He was married at the time to a very distinguished lady, selling off bits of her family's antiques. She was quite a bit older than he, and surprisingly wealthy, in spite of the war. He was a charmer. She died."

"He married her for her money, then?"

"I did not say that, but of course, he got nothing in the end, or very little compared to what was there. You know the French. Her family made certain it stayed with them. He took what he could get and set himself up in America. I can't imagine what the immigration people were thinking at the time."

"I haven't met him," Margaret said, "although his factotum is on his way to becoming my devoted servant. He might prove to be useful in fending off the interior designers working at the house."

"Those designers are creatures from a different universe, if you ask me. Oh, they're not always bad one-on-one, but when they're in their designing mode, protecting their creations, there's no telling what they'll do. I remember once when I loaned some really beautiful pieces of Ming to—what is her name? The lady Reagan or Bush or somebody sent to Scandinavia and then there was the trouble about the lingonberries."

"Madame Ambassador, Mrs. Corbell. What about your Ming?" Actually Margaret was more curious now to learn about the celebrated lingonberry affair.

"It was for a showhouse like yours, but the volunteer ladies who were supposed to be keeping an eye on the rooms allowed my pieces to find their way into visitors' handbags. Or perhaps they fancied them themselves. Madame, of course, refused to compensate me for my losses, and she had no insurance. She turned rather vicious in the end. Well, my dear, don't let me discourage you. Have fun."

"Bedros . . ." Margaret looked at him hard.

"Something is troubling you." He beamed at her, not from pleasure but because that was his way.

"It's De Vere," she said. "He said he'd been to see you. Something's amiss. He's . . . he's not there anymore."

"There?"

"We've been together for seven years now, and it's been good. Oh, he natters on about how I shouldn't get involved in these dreadful murders, and I quite agree. No human being other than a policeman should encounter more than perhaps one murder victim in a lifetime, and moreover shouldn't then be expected to discover the perpetrator. It's . . . unnatural. But it's not my fault. Things just seem to happen, and people will talk to me, and perhaps I have a gift for figuring out how relationships fit together and seeing the crack that causes someone to murder another. But Sam is getting more and more distant. I know he's thinking of leaving the police, but if he does, what happens to us?"

Kasparian gazed up at the ceiling, then fixed his eye on the Kuan Yin statue—supposedly a symbol of good fortune. He stroked the chessman, pursed his lips, and frowned. "I don't believe, from what he's said, that De Vere plans to marry again. You need more security, I think, than he's willing to give you. Maybe you should think about seeing other men."

Margaret conjured up the image of Eddie Leone's face, awash with dumb infatuation.

"There aren't that many choices," she said. "Besides, Sam is . . ." Perhaps she did love Sam De Vere, although she seldom thought about it. However, the idea of involving herself with another man was entirely unacceptable. That had to mean something.

"It could be, my dear, that Sam himself is feeling . . . restless. Might he have other . . . lady friends about whom you know nothing?"

She imagined Sam De Vere courting an unknown healthy, loving, domesticated woman, pretty and good-natured, who would revel in decorating a house in a small town in New Jersey, and would be happy having the neighbors in for tea and grubbing in the garden, which would put forth magnificent flowers and plump red Jersey tomatoes, peas, and the inevitable zucchini, and then cooking gourmet meals day after day to please her beloved. An amiable dog, a reserved cat, an adorable child or two to ferry about in the station wagon to school and lessons.

She didn't see herself in the part. Depressingly, she saw herself tied to city life, escorted to glittering affairs by the likes of Giovanni Millennia or Bobby Henley, surrounded by brittle, witty conversation. Then she saw herself guiding imperious society ladies to select the right fabrics, and averting decor disaster by diplomatically steering them away from tasteless furnishings. She saw herself at endless, wine-soaked lunches surrounded by shrill women who chattered on about their awful husbands, their divine lovers, and their social triumphs.

"Why would you think De Vere has other girlfriends?" It was difficult for her to get the words out. "Has he mentioned . . . ?"

Kasparian shrugged. "I know men, being one myself for seventy or more years. Sam is an attractive man, out in the world, meeting new people every day. Even in the world of crime, there are many interesting diversions. But I know nothing."

"What should I do?" Margaret was pleading with her old friend to guide her through this treacherous patch of her life. She didn't want to lose De Vere to a perky waitress/actress or to one of the flashy women he met on the street. "You do know something. But don't worry. I don't care to know, so I won't ask you to betray confidences." She paused at the door. "Let me know if you decide to reopen the shop. I suspect my consultant job with Giovanni will quickly lose its charm."

"Tell De Vere what you want," Kasparian said. "My advice."

Margaret caught an express bus back to Manhattan. En route she stared out the window as the nice, orderly, old-fashioned apartment buildings in Kasparian's neighborhood gradually yielded to the shambles of the South Bronx, past the shabby tenements, and the active street life, the aimless young men clustered at the doors of corner bodegas, clutching brown paper bags concealing bottles of Corona or Red Stripe beer. By the time the bus was passing Central Park and the magnificent apartment houses on Fifth Avenue, she was dozing, but then some inner alarm jerked her awake, and she got off the bus at the express stop nearest the street where the Gilpin house was located. Giovanni had mentioned that he might be there most of the day, deciding on his plan of attack for stripping and repainting his room. She didn't imagine he'd expect her to hoist a paintbrush and start slapping on a coat of semigloss, but perhaps there would be a chore for her to do.

Then she decided she'd had enough of the Gilpins and showhouses for one day. She went home to read about Renaissance art.

Chapter 11

*T*he following day, Margaret felt she ought to put in an appearance at the showhouse.

When she arrived, the front door was wide-open. In the foyer, a dark-haired young tough was sitting at a card table on a folding chair. He looked up none too happily from the motorcycle magazine he was reading and gave Margaret an insolent once-over.

"Private house," he said. "No admittance."

"I'm working with Mrs. Anton on the showhouse," Margaret informed him, and when that had no apparent effect, she added, "And Eddie Leone."

"Oh, yeah. He's upstairs with a bunch of those . . . decorator guys." The youth was apparently not yet attuned to the delicate aesthetic sensibilities of the interior-design crowd.

"Is Mrs. Anton here? She's blond, tall, nice clothes."

"These dames all look the same to me. I wouldn't know the one you're looking for." He jerked a thumb toward the stairs. "Eddie's probably on the third floor, but you got to walk up. The elevator's shut down."

A burst of sound came from the back of the house, the whine of an electric saw, the pounding of a drill.

"What's going on?" she asked.

"They're partitioning one of the big rooms to make two," the kid said. "Eddie would be there if he's not upstairs." He started leafing through the pages of his magazine.

She strolled toward the back of the house and peered into the room that had been the old dining room. Three men were raising a Sheetrock wall and nailing it to two-by-four studs while Godfrey Helms looked on and provided a running commentary.

"Look, you're putting the door to the kitchen in the wrong place! I want the door to be four inches more to the left. Exactly four inches. I have a divine little chest that I'm putting on the right side of the door. I need that space. And please take extra care not to damage the ceiling, I don't want the plasterwork harmed. You! I'm talking to *you*!" One of the workmen paused and deliberately prodded a remnant of two-by-four on the floor with the toe of his work boot.

"You talking to *me*, man?" he asked lazily. "And I ain't goin' anywhere near your ceiling." Then he narrowed his eyes in an effort to stare Godfrey down.

Godfrey looked away and sighed mightily. "Oh, really." He caught sight of Margaret. "Lady Margaret, welcome to my little room. Mind the rubbish these people have not seen fit to dispose of." The workmen stopped hammering and looked around at him. Godfrey huffed and puffed out his cheeks and directed his full attention to Margaret, thus avoiding their murderous looks.

"I'm considering something a bit different for this room," he said. "Tell me what you think. First a color that will simply slay them. The right shade of geranium or coral with all the polished wood will be sensational. Of course, those damned girls have taken away my windows at the back with their kitchen nonsense. There's a lovely little square of garden out in back, and tall windows. I did so want to bring the outdoors into my room. Now they have it." He pouted. The workmen exchanged long-suffering glances and picked up their tools.

"I'm sure you'll do a wonderful job," Margaret said. "Why not make your own outdoors? With some sort of clever lighting?" she suggested.

Godfrey was thrilled at the idea. "You're a genius! I have it now!" He was suddenly out of his funk, gesturing dramatically at the blank, windowless left-hand wall. "I'll do a window treatment on that wall, closed draperies, some lovely sort of fabric from Stroheim, and then some clever concealed lighting behind so that it will appear as though the sun is setting outside and the curtains have just been drawn. With the chandelier lighted over the dining table, it will work perfectly." He studied the ceiling. "I suppose one of these louts can handle the rewiring."

The two kitchen girls bounced in from the main hall. The dark-haired one carried a big sketchpad, and the other was festooned with tape measures and was hauling a pile of swatch books and catalogs in a huge carryall. She stopped and surveyed the newly erected wall.

"Hi, guys," she said to the workmen, who seemed to appreciate a reasonably positive acknowledgment of their existence. "Godfrey, love, you're going to have them move the door way over to the right. We're putting a twelve-foot-long cabinet against the wall in the other room in our kitchen, and it will block half the doorway."

"Can't," was all Godfrey said, but Margaret heard him mutter under his breath, "And won't."

"Come on, sweetie," the other girl said, "be nice and let us have our wall."

"I need *my* wall right where it is," he said. "I have a lovely—"

"I'm sure it's adorable," the girl with the carry-all said.

"Look," Godfrey said, and his tone was not conciliatory. "You've got the windows and the light, and far more space than you need or deserve, so get off my back."

The dark-haired girl smiled soothingly. "Do remember, Godfrey, if you don't move the door to the right, your table and stuff will have to be on the far side of the room so it won't interfere with traffic to the kitchen. Visitors will be going through a door that's practically in the middle of the wall. It's going to be cramped for you, unless you want your table to block the route. How much easier it would be if the traffic was kept close to the right-hand wall, but oh dear, then the door would have to be moved farther to the right. Well, it's your decision. Let us know."

The two girls picked their way through the scattered pieces of Sheetrock and into their kitchen-to-be.

Godfrey cleared his throat and pointed to one of the workmen. "You there. Yes, you. I want the door to be moved all the way to the right, at right angles to the wall." The workman opened his mouth. "No arguments," Godfrey said. "I'm paying for this." He turned to Margaret. "My 'stuff' indeed!" He shrugged microscopically. "I hate to admit it, but she's right. We don't allow the visitors to roam all about our rooms, although it doesn't appear to matter much in a kitchen, but in a room like mine, things could get broken, and people do steal; they might upset the dog. It's better to have a direct route from room to room that doesn't interfere with the decor."

Margaret had had about enough of Godfrey's fussing. "Is Gloria in the house today?" she asked. "I haven't seen her in four days."

"I saw her earlier. There are a number of people around upstairs. Women from the committee, designers, painters . . ."

"I think I'll just see if I can locate her," Margaret said.

Out in the hall, she heard vague noises from above, murmured voices, and an occasional thump. A man in painter's overalls came through the front door, hauling a short ladder. He was followed by a helper who carried a gallon of paint over each arm. The guard boy paid little attention to them. Then Kenneth appeared, laden down with wicker baskets and a bolt of sprigged muslin.

Hearing a faint mechanical hum from the back near the dining room, Margaret tilted her head to listen. The elevator, of course, even though it was supposed to be shut down. She followed the painters up the stairs, but before she had taken half a dozen steps, a piercing scream ripped through the house, followed by another and another. The painters halted suddenly and looked up. The guard boy abandoned his reading and started for the stairs. Margaret didn't hesitate, but pushed past the painters and ran up the stairs well ahead of the boy, who in any case was not displaying any particular urgency.

Arriving on the second-floor landing, she saw Bobby Henley hovering nervously by the door to the library. The substantial form of Madame Ambassador emerged from the drawing room farther down the landing. Margaret continued to the third floor, where she found Giovanni and Kenneth looking disturbed and confused.

"What happened?" she asked breathlessly.

Giovanni shrugged. "Fourth floor. I think Gloria went up there."

Margaret bit her lip and continued bravely on up the stairs. No one followed her. On the landing, she discovered Gloria crumpled in a heap on the floor, with Eddie Leone on his knees beside her. Margaret knelt down beside him and took one of Gloria's icy hands.

"Gloria."

Eddie looked at Margaret with relief tinged with adoration. "I don't know what happened," he said. "I came upstairs on the elevator. I opened the door just as she was coming out of one of the rooms over there. She saw me and started screaming bloody murder. Then she fainted. Or something."

At that moment Gloria opened her eyes, sat up, and immediately launched into an apology. She had nothing, however, to say about the cause of her fainting, but Margaret noticed a look of fear as her eyes flickered from face to face in the anxious circle that surrounded her.

"I think I'll have Eddie drive me at once to the Villa d'Este," she announced. "I feel a little shaky."

"Let me come with you," Margaret said.

"I'll come, too," Bobby said. "Darling, you gave us *such* a fright." The other decorators, hovering uncertainly on the landing, murmured agreement. Margaret noted that Godfrey Helms had not been sufficiently alarmed to investigate along with the others. Perhaps the workmen had wrestled him to the ground and bound him with duct tape to quiet his endless prattling.

"It was just a silly accident," Gloria said. "No harm done. Please go back to your work, I know you have so much to do. I'll be fine. Yes, Margaret, I'd like you to come along, but not you, Bobby. I couldn't bear to think I was keeping you from more important tasks."

"Well, yes. My painters are here, but I'm not ready for them at all," Bobby said. "The floors aren't finished yet, and I can't have the dust mucking up the paint. Promise you'll take care of yourself, Gloria."

"Thanks for your concern, sweetie," she said.

Chapter 12

Gloria and Margaret, trailed by Eddie, proceeded down the stairs and out of the house. Gloria said softly to Margaret, "Don't ask anything, don't talk about it, until we're alone at the d'Este." She nodded her head in Eddie's direction. "Eddie, be a dear and don't mention this to Mr. Anton. I don't want to worry him. I'll tell him about it later."

"Yes, ma'am," Eddie said, and opened the door of the car.

Margaret couldn't help thinking that there wasn't much sharing in the Anton marriage, if each spouse had to worry all the time about Eddie Leone repeating what the other had said.

Eddie dropped them at the hotel, where a handsomely uniformed doorman opened the car door and ushered them into the building.

"The boss is out someplace with Mr. Centner," Eddie said. "You want I should find him? I can call him on the car phone."

"No," Gloria said, "I'm fine, and I have Lady Margaret with me. I just had a dizzy spell, and you startled me when you appeared so suddenly from the elevator."

She seemed quite calm now, although she was silent as the quiet elevator carried them up to the twelfth floor.

Margaret followed her down a short hallway carpeted in a lovely shade of sea-foam green instead of the usual garish dark flower pattern that hotels use to hide the wear of foot traffic.

"It's not much of a place," Gloria said as she unlocked the door. "Although Carolyn Sue did a terrific job of renovating the hotel itself. Godfrey advised her, since he has such a name as a hotel decorator." They walked into a large glaringly white sitting room, with a curved white leather sofa, a lounge chair that looked too elaborate for the space, and a big round glass coffee table in the center. A brilliant round red area rug and a vase of red flowers exactly matching the rug provided a distinctive touch of color.

"We don't even have a real kitchen," Gloria said, "just a little refrigerator and a stove top with a couple of burners to boil water. And the microwave. Peter prefers to eat out, and since I'm not much of a cook, that's fine with me. My children would have starved if we hadn't had a wonderful cook. Katya, my grandfather's old housekeeper, came to Leland and me after her husband Boris died. She's with me still, although only on a part-time basis. She's getting on in years."

"She knew your brother Eric, then."

"Oh yes. She was fond of Eric. He was her pet, and she was there at the house when he died. Downstairs."

"I see." Margaret noticed that Gloria was becoming distracted as she bustled about offering coffee, tea, wine, sherry. Margaret declined them all. Finally Gloria settled on the white sofa with a tall glass full of ice and either water or vodka. Margaret suspected the latter. As she watched Gloria settle down she puzzled over how to speak with Katya in private, and realized that this would require frequent visits to Gloria's pied-à-terre, which she was reluctant to make. She couldn't, however, just come right out and ask to meet the woman. Gloria would quite rightly expect an explanation.

"I don't normally drink much," Gloria said, "after what I went through with my mother. Dougie seems to have the family disease now, but I needed something to pick me up after this business today."

"What about today?" Margaret asked, curious to know what had caused Gloria's screams and her collapse on the landing.

"I was in a rather fragile state to begin with," Gloria said, "All that bickering and more bickering. They're not redecorating Versailles, for heaven's sake. And then Bobby and Godfrey had been going on and on about dogs. I told them absolutely not, but do you think they heard me? Not a word." She stared at her glass and said softly, "My grandfather had a lovely Irish setter there for years. Morgan used to lie in front of the fireplace in the library and never caused a problem to anyone. Boris or Katya, sometimes Grandfather even, would take him down the street to Central Park for a run. Later it was just a stroll, as Morgan became rather arthritic in his later years." Gloria seemed momentarily lost in her happy old memories.

"What else about today?" Margaret asked, hating to interrupt her reverie.

"What? Why, nothing else." Gloria opened her eyes wide, acting out innocent puzzlement.

"Gloria, you started screaming bloody murder, and then I find you half-conscious on the floor. I think there must be something else." Margaret was trying not to become impatient with her.

Gloria leaned back on the sofa and closed her eyes. "Eddie startled me, coming out of the elevator suddenly like that. I was just looking through the rooms on that floor, and I thought I heard someone moving about. I thought it might be one of the decorators, although we decided against doing the rooms up there for the showhouse. I got to the doorway of what used to be Hannah's office. I heard the elevator, and turned toward it, then I . . ." She started to breathe heavily, almost gasping for air, and put her hand to her breast as though willing her heart to beat more slowly.

"What?" Margaret asked.

"I heard someone behind me in the office. I froze. I didn't know what to do. Then someone put hands around my throat with the thumbs pressing against the side of my neck, choking me. I was just barely able to scream. The hands went away." She sounded very shaky, and Margaret hoped she wasn't going to become hysterical.

"Then you saw Eddie come out of the elevator?"

Gloria was suddenly still, her breathing regular. She had a vaguely puzzled look. "I don't remember," she said. "I saw someone, it might have been Eddie, but I only remember waking up and seeing him kneeling beside me."

"Could Eddie have been the person who put his hands on your neck?"

"I don't know. I don't think so, and why would he? Whoever it was, was trying to choke the life out of me."

"Do you remember anything—sight, sound, smell, anything?"

Gloria seemed to be withdrawing into herself, thinking, a turn of events Margaret found worrisome. She couldn't help but wonder if Gloria hadn't simply imagined that someone tried to choke her.

Gloria shook her head. "Nothing. Except . . . Mother's perfume. Joy. But I must have imagined it. That part of the house always terrifies me."

"I can understand that," Margaret said soothingly.

"Not just Eric. Because of what it meant. Everything had seemed all right before that day, and then everything wasn't right. And has never been since, except for Peter. All I know is that someone was up there and caused Eric to fall."

Margaret remembered De Vere's question about Poppy's alleged "proof," which had made it possible for her to blackmail old Douglas Gilpin.

"But who was it?"

"Don't you think I've tried to figure that out over the years? For a while," Gloria said slowly, "I believed it was my mother. Can you imagine that? Thinking my own mother was responsible for the death of her own child? I couldn't live easily with that." Margaret could hear the emotion welling up in her voice, but she went on. "I did terribly at boarding school my first term. I couldn't concentrate, couldn't learn the simplest fact in history or read a whole book for English class. But I couldn't go home to Mother and Daddy, not with what I believed. Eric was gone, Dougie was back at Yale. Hannah had gone away with Monsieur Crouzat, and Grandfather was ill. Then Grandfather died, and a couple of months later, Mother was gone.

"When she killed herself, I was sure she'd done it out of guilt for killing Eric, but I couldn't tell anyone. So I just soldiered on at school, and went to stay with Aunt Flora at her place in Maine for the summer, or with friends from school for the holidays. I had no family to speak of by then, because Daddy wasn't especially warm and loving. That was his way. When I finished high school, I went to college, and met Leland. We got married and I had two lovely children. Then Leland left me, and even though I made sure he paid for that betrayal, my life was still miserable."

"So you don't really know who it was who might have caused your brother's accident."

"I don't know anything," Gloria said. "I don't know why Eric was up there on the fourth floor. He said he had a joke to tell me, so I went up. I was looking for Hannah to say good-bye, but she had gone. Dougie was playing pool in the basement, Mother was somewhere about waiting for luncheon to be served. Boris and Katya were down below getting luncheon ready. I left Grandfather in the library. Hannah showed up later, but I don't know where she was at the time it happened. Margaret, I just don't know anything for sure, and it's made me crazy."

Margaret felt a pang of sympathy for Gloria. She had lived so many years with the knowledge that her brother had been murdered, wondering about who had killed him, and this despite the announcement of the police that the death had been accidental. Margaret herself was not convinced that it was anything more, that Eric hadn't simply taken a risk and fallen, a typical teenage boy who knew it all and believed himself invincible. Or perhaps Gloria knew more than she admitted. Perhaps it was true, like Poppy said, that Dougie killed Eric.

"It wasn't Dougie today, was it?" Margaret asked gently.

"Of course not! It was—" She stopped, and Margaret waited. "The hands were strong, but soft. Like a woman's almost."

If Madame Ambassador was sufficiently irate about being denied her preferred room, she might feel compelled to punish the cause of her defeat. But surely Bobby Henley was a more likely object of her wrath. Still, anyone who could turn lingonberries into an international crisis was a woman to be reckoned with. And then there was Angela. . . .

"You will stand by me, won't you?" Gloria asked forlornly. With her careful makeup in ruins and her assurance gone, Gloria looked frail and vulnerable. "I'm very wealthy," she said.

"How nice for you," Margaret said, "but it doesn't matter much to me one way or the other." She wondered if Gloria thought wealth lifted her into the rarefied realms of not-very-wealthy English aristocrats like Margaret herself. Well, those realms were crowded nowadays.

"I didn't mean anything relative to you," Gloria said. "It's just that . . . people seem to think the money's there for them. Christine, bless her, is quite self-sufficient, although I have helped her out from time to time. It's costly to take all those trips to Mexico for her work, and she has to hire local people to help her dig, and so on."

Gloria actually smiled, and then started to laugh, high-pitched and maybe a touch hysterical. "Christine had a price for being on my committee. She wanted me to buy her some nice . . . nice clothes . . . so she wouldn't embarrass me." Tears were gathering at the corners of Gloria's eyes. "A cocktail dress, she said, and a nice suit and shoes. Oh, Christine . . ." She was almost sobbing now. "She's a lovely girl, she'd never embarrass me, and you'd like Angus, too. So serious and intelligent. Well, she will have her clothes. And then there's Ricky, who always needs money, but I don't begrudge him. You know how young men are."

Margaret knew well, being aware of Paul Castrocani's continual efforts to persuade his mother—who was far richer than Gloria, she was sure—to subsidize a lavish lifestyle.

"That's a mother's job, though, isn't it? To indulge her children, up to a point."

Having heard from several people that Gloria had helped to bankroll her husband's business ventures, Margaret was hoping that Gloria would move on to the subject of spousal demands, but unfortunately, she remained silent on the subject of Peter Anton.

"I've had to loan money to Dougie from time to time. Pauline is more expensive than his first wife was . . . is. He seems to feel that because he didn't inherit as much as I did from Grandfather and Mother, he's entitled to ask me. He never pays me back." She stood up and looked around the suite. "I pay for this. Peter thought it would be a good idea to have this place in the city." She shrugged. "I suppose he is right. He often stays in the city overnight, even when I'm not with him." She seemed downcast when she added, "I know he brings women here. You notice the little signs. The strand of hair in the bathroom sink, the traces of powder, the hint of a fragrance ..." She stopped abruptly and again started to breathe heavily.

"Gloria?" Margaret's tone was as worried as she felt.

"It's nothing," Gloria said. "I was remembering something about that day."

Margaret didn't need to ask of which day she was speaking.

"I remember perfume. I mentioned it to you," she went on. "Up there on the fourth-floor landing, with Eric in his red-and-tan jacket at the door to the stairs. Joy—it was a very popular scent back then, immediately recognizable as a sign of good, expensive taste. Nowadays, with all these Calvins and Elizabeths and celebrity scents, it doesn't have the cachet it once did, but to the ladies of my mother's generation ..."

She trailed off. Of course, Gloria's mother would have worn Joy as her signature perfume. Margaret's own mother had been scented with lavender and the rose petals from Priam's Priory's rose gardens, sprinkled in drawers of silky undergarments. None of that fancy French *parfum* for the Countess of Brayfield. Then Margaret wondered what scent Hannah Garber had preferred.

"Do you have a husband?" Gloria asked suddenly.

"I had one once, some years ago," Margaret said, taken aback. "He was as poor a choice for me as I was for him. We parted amicably. I see him every year or two when I'm in England. He's very happily remarried. I presently have a close ... person." She didn't know what to call De Vere, or whether he even was still the person she was close to.

"Yes, I'd forgotten that Poppy mentioned you kept company with a policeman."

"It's not serious, really," Margaret said. "We're good friends and enjoy each other's company." That was a very sketchy picture of their relationship, but Margaret didn't care to indulge in cozy girl-talk complaints and problems with her man. Margaret reminded herself to call De Vere later to ask when Paul and the lovely Georgina were arriving. It did seem unlikely that Paul would want to leave the tropical pleasures of Boucan to return to New York in February. The island's version of Carnival was coming up soon, and he wouldn't want to miss that.

"Poppy also said that you have, well, solved some murders."

"Mostly by accident," Margaret said, "when there was no one else to do it."

Gloria was silent for a time. Then she went to the drinks cabinet and poured an inch of Stolichnaya into her glass, dropped in ice cubes and a slice of lime, and splashed in some seltzer. "Nothing for you?" she asked, and Margaret shook her head.

Gloria sat again on her white sofa and Margaret watched as she sipped from her glass. "I want you to help me," she said finally.

"I'll do the best I can," Margaret promised, willfully misunderstanding. "I don't really know all that much about putting together a decorator showhouse, but it seems to be just a matter of keeping the designers happy and getting the paying customers in. I'll help Terry Thompson with the journal if she needs me, and Dianne is a whiz at publicity. I have long lists of people to send invitations to for the opening gala. I'll even address envelopes and guard rooms to keep the visitors from walking off with the odd candelabra or vase."

Gloria was not to be put off by this ruse. "I mean, I want you to help me learn who murdered my brother. And who seems to be trying to kill me," she added. She seemed to have put her emotions to rest for the moment.

"I don't think I can do that," Margaret said. "I'm not a trained investigator, just a displaced Brit trying to maintain a decent lifestyle and muddle through my personal life."

"But people have said you've solved . . . I could pay you for your trouble," Gloria quickly offered.

Margaret shook her head. "Hire a professional, if you like. I am not the person you need."

"What about your friend with the police?"

"Mr. De Vere doesn't freelance," Margaret said, "and besides, he breaks out in hives at the mere mention of the Social Register. In any event, the police must have investigated your brother's death thoroughly at the time. If there was the slightest suspicion of foul play, they would have pursued it to its logical conclusion."

Gloria gazed at a spot in space above Margaret's head. "I'm sure Grandfather and Daddy simply put a stop to further investigation. For Mother's sake, and . . . you know, the family name. Grandfather was able to pull as many strings as a puppeteer. I mean, my brother Dougie did something terrible once. He got drunk up at Yale and had a car accident, where somebody died. It was entirely his fault, but nothing came of it. Grandfather saw to it." Gloria suddenly fixed Margaret with a terrified stare. "Please, Margaret, help me."

"Only if you are honest with me. Did you do it?"

"What? Hurt Eric?" Gloria seemed shocked at such a notion, even offended. "Don't be silly. He was an awful little boy, but you always grow up thinking your brothers are awful. And sometimes they are." .

Margaret thought about her brother David. He had not been a perfect sibling when he was young, but he'd turned out all right. At the very least, he was being decently selective about choosing a wife to take their mother's place as the mistress of Priam's Priory. Margaret said, "When I was a teenager, I thought my brother was pretty impossible, but we're fairly good friends now. He's keeping up the family estate, and all he needs to do is marry and produce an heir so the Priory and the title won't go to some Australian cousin, as has been known to happen. I do understand about brothers."

"You will help me," Gloria said. "I know you will. You can talk to people and they'll pay attention. Dougie, Hannah, Katya even. They were all somewhere about that day. Katya will be thrilled to talk to a real titled lady. She and Boris were quite the snobs. And you'll be at Grandfather's house often on show-house business, so you can look around to your heart's content. I'll help as much as I can. Dougie will, too, if you catch him in a good mood, and even Leland. But," she added sternly, "you must promise to never, never say a word about this to Angela. She'd spread the news faster than she can charge a gown at Bergdorf's. I wouldn't be surprised if she's been plotting to murder me for years because of all the money I got from

Leland in the divorce." Gloria grinned. "Besides, she thinks I've put Leland in my will. It's not true, but who cares if she thinks it? You can start tomorrow."

"I haven't agreed to anything," Margaret said. "I really can't." She was thinking about Angela Forsythe.

Gloria placed her glass carefully on the table and folded her arms across her chest. "You will." Although she spoke mildly, it was clearly no longer a question or a plea. She was taking charge, no arguments allowed.

Margaret looked at her, a middle-aged woman whose years were showing in this nonpublic moment, whose bright pink suit seemed too youthful, but who was still able to use her "little ways" to her own advantage. The chairlady expected her minions to hop to it.

"I've spent the last forty years having people look at me and imagine that I murdered my own brother. They don't dare say it out loud, but I know what they're thinking. I'm tired," she said. "I've always tried to be a good person, and I didn't murder anyone."

"I'm sure you didn't," Margaret said, but she wasn't at all sure. She was also not convinced that someone was trying to murder Gloria. But if the woman enjoyed the imagined threat, what good would it do to question its reality?

"Well, that's settled," Gloria said happily. "I'll arrange for you to talk with anyone you wish. Now, what do you think of the house? It's going to be superb, the decorators are all such professionals."

Margaret shrugged. "Godfrey Helms and the kitchen girls are certain to come to blows. I have never seen a door moved so many times in such a short space of time. Of course, it's equally possible that the construction men may be driven to take lethal action."

"Them." Gloria waved them away. "They're Eddie's boys. He'll keep them under control. Eddie seems to have a . . . special affection for you, Margaret. You do appear to attract . . ."

"The lower orders?" She could easily read Gloria's thoughts. First a policeman, then a sort of blue-collar guy. "My accent seems to appeal to a certain type, but the effect doesn't last long. And it can't hurt to have Eddie on my side. Our side."

"He's on my side only by default," Gloria said. "He belongs to Peter and Centner."

"Centner?"

"My husband's partner. The one who finds all the terrific deals that Peter needs a little extra money to close. He actually suggested to Peter that he charge me a fee for the use of *my* house!"

Hmm. Husbands and money at last. "I'll have to think about this . . . that day," Margaret said. "I can't promise anything."

"We'll meet at the house tomorrow. Is eleven too early for you? I can show you all around the fourth floor where it happened."

"And check if Bobby has found the right shade of green for his walls and rug, and whether the wood can be stripped down successfully. Will Godfrey have decided on coral or geranium for his walls, and has the Door Question been settled at last? Will Bobby's golden retriever be able to coexist with Godfrey's Irish wolfhound?" Margaret covered her mouth to hide a fit of giggles.

"Why are you laughing?" Gloria asked crossly. "These are important questions, except for those damned dogs. Do you know how big an Irish wolfhound is?"

"I do, and it was the dogs I was laughing about," Margaret said. "I was imagining Madame Ambassador in a fine fury confronting Godfrey after his decorative wolfhound has tracked mud across the carpet of her lovely lady's retreat. 'Mr. Helms, these are the footprints of a gigantic hound. . . .' I do hope I am present to hear the words."

Chapter 13

"*Poppy*, Gloria Anton expects me to look into her brother's death. That was nearly forty years ago." Margaret had awoken the next day to the realization of the enormity of what she had promised to do. A call to Poppy Dill was her first action.

"And very good of you to agree," Poppy said. "Can I help?"

"Yes, you can," Margaret said. "I'm meeting Gloria at the Gilpin house at eleven. I want to see you before then. I can be at your apartment in half an hour, at nine."

Poppy didn't argue. All she said was, "I think it's too short notice to get Hannah here."

"I don't want to see her now," Margaret said, "but I'm sure the occasion will arise."

"She's only here for another two days," Poppy said. "I'll see that she's available to talk with you the day after tomorrow."

"Listen," Margaret said, "somebody attacked Gloria at the Gilpin house. Or at least that's what she claims. She was in a terrible state when I saw her."

"Tsk," Poppy said. "I'd take a close look at the husband."

"But you said he was quite charming, you sounded as though you liked him."

"Ah, but I know human nature, and I know these people. . . ." Poppy let her words trail off cryptically. What she meant was that she knew many a tale about poorish husbands who coveted the assets of their wealthy wives. At least that was what Margaret was thinking.

After Poppy, she dialed De Vere, and was surprised that he was still at home.

"Paul said he'd be in at the end of the week," De Vere said, "for two or three days. Then he's off to Texas to introduce Georgina to his mother and step-father, then to Rome to have her meet his father, his paternal aunts and uncles, cousins, and the rest of the black/white Roman nobility. Then they're going to England to see her family. Eventually, one supposes they'll make it to the marriage ceremony. I'll probably be evicted if the happy couple wants this place, seeing as it belongs to Carolyn Sue."

"Well . . ." Margaret hesitated. "There's room here with me if you're out on the street. Nothing permanent, I mean, but you always have a place. It's not as conve-nient for you as Paul's apartment, but at least you wouldn't have to waste time right off looking for something. I know you always have your parents' place in New Jersey, but the commute isn't all that easy. . . ."

"Don't babble, Margaret. Paul hasn't put me out yet, and knowing him as I do, I'm still not convinced that he'll actually set himself up with a wife and all that it entails. But thanks for the offer, there's no one I'd rather impose on. And you know perfectly well that the

New Jersey suburban life isn't for me. Shopping malls, gardens, station wagons, grass to mow . . . I had enough pressure about that kind of life from my first wife. She thought it was paradise."

Ah, the first wife. The one who De Vere said couldn't take being married to a policeman. His first marriage had not been a success. "My idea of country living is that little bit of England I indulge in every couple of years," she said.

"Good girl." De Vere said. "Let's worry about my homeless state when it happens. Are you managing all right with the showhouse and the so-called murder?"

"I promised to look into it," Margaret said, "but," she added hastily before he could comment, "I'm not going to look too hard. As for the showhouse, I think I'm going to be dealing with a lot of Martha Stewart wannabes, but they're not bad, as long as they can get the painters to match their paint chips. The dogs may be a problem, and the actors. And Godfrey's monks, certainly."

De Vere laughed. It was good to hear. "Monks? I honestly don't want to know more about that until much later. Am I being insensitive to your concerns?"

"Not at all," Margaret said happily. "Unless you have very strong opinions about coral walls versus geranium."

"Not in this lifetime, babe," he said. "What do you say we have dinner tonight, here or at your place? And then spend a nice quiet evening watching television. We could catch a rerun of *Murder She Wrote.* . . ."

"Chinese," Margaret said promptly, quite pleased they would not be served by a forward young waitress.

"At my apartment, with real ice cream—no low-fat, no-fat fake stuff."

"It's a date," De Vere said. "You're a very restful woman. I like that. I'll be there before eight. I'll stop at Vision of the Lotus and pick up the food."

"I'll be here, chopsticks at the ready. Have them do lobster in garlic sauce, whether in or out of season."

"Dry sautéed beef."

"Cold jellyfish. Scallion pancakes."

Margaret rushed to put herself together so as to reach Poppy's apartment at the time she'd promised. She made it.

Poppy's boudoir was unchanged from her previous visit, although no Hannah sat in the interview chair this morning. Poppy was again garbed in fluffy pink garments, although today she sat at her ancient typewriter.

"Margaret dear, just sit yourself down, or make yourself some tea. I have a column to finish that's going to get picked up in half an hour. They're talking about fixing me up with a computer that'll talk to the ones at the paper. Frightening thought for an old woman."

Poppy busied herself with her column for a moment. Margaret said, "Now Gloria's saying that someone is trying to kill her."

Poppy continued to type away for a time. Then she turned to face Margaret, but she remained deep in thought. "Who would want to kill Gloria? I mean, besides Peter, and I doubt he would. He would be suspected right off, and I understand she gives him anything he wants. People like her—except for Angela, of course. I could imagine Angela plotting murder, but I doubt she would get much beyond thinking about it. She's not the brightest bulb in the candelabra, but she's always resented that huge settlement Gloria got from Leland. I've told her time and again that that's one of the drawbacks of luring away another woman's husband."

"I suspect Gloria's just imagining things," Margaret said, "except for the incident yesterday." Then she had to explain the scene on the fourth floor and the person who allegedly tried to choke Gloria. "Let's leave Gloria's fantasies for the moment. Tell me about Eric."

"I don't like to betray confidences, but under the circumstances, I suppose I must. . . . First of all, I never knew Eric, he was dead by the time I got mixed up with the Gilpins, but he was not a nice boy. And Dougie is not an especially nice person, not then and not now."

"Yes, Dougie. I met him briefly. He admitted his youthful affair with Hannah. He did not quite admit to marriage."

"You do understand that money was—*is* very important to Hannah, and she thought Dougie stood to get a lot fairly soon. She thought that fake Frenchman Crouzat was pretty well-fixed, too, but I warned her he wasn't. He was what we used to call a bounder."

"And he bounded. Gloria says they were divorced."

"If they were ever married," Poppy said knowingly.

"Did Hannah say they weren't? Dougie said they were."

"Well, that would have been quite a scandal for the Gilpins, if they had been," Poppy said, but she continued to type her column and leave Margaret to wonder what sort of enduring scandal could arise for the family from the marriage of the old man's secretary and his granddaughter's French teacher.

"I must run over to the showhouse," Margaret said. "I don't like the idea of Gloria roaming around there. Especially if you're not going to tell me whatever else you know."

"I'm not," Poppy said. "And it will be all right. It was all so long ago, and these things pass. I've known far worse. How is the house coming?"

"Enthusiasm seems high, although that may fade in time," Margaret said. "There's some temperament evident."

The house was open as before. Today as she went in, a youth high up on a ladder was measuring the windows while Alfred Knox, the decorator who was to handle the ground-floor entrance foyer, looked on. The old bedsheets were piled on the floor, ready to do duty as painters' dropcloths. The smell of paint was heavy.

A wrenlike woman peered out of one of the small side rooms off the hallway. Margaret remembered that she was renowned for her trompe l'oeil, and was planning on painting views of the English countryside on the walls of her room. The two kitchen girls bounded along the hallway, chattering of tile floors.

"Is Gloria here?" Margaret asked Alfred, a white-haired patrician in blue blazer and gray trousers. He looked as though he should be on the deck of a yacht on Long Island Sound.

"Haven't seen her," he said. "Bobby Henley is here, though, and you always see the two of them together."

The guard boy didn't give Margaret a second look

today, so she went up to the next floor. Bobby was in his room with several men who were busy refinishing the wood paneling. Bobby was wearing old jeans and a plaid shirt, and was actually assisting in the stripping process. He had a white mask over his nose and mouth, and wore safety glasses.

"Gloria's upstairs, I think," he said, pulling the mask down under his chin. "Simply everyone seems to be here today. Giovanni was asking for you. Don't stand around here, the fumes are dreadful. But my floors are finished—and dry. I stayed until all hours so I could get on with the paneling and put the painters to work today. I've booked a pricey photographer to shoot the room for an ad, even if I change things before the show."

Margaret went on up to the third floor, found Giovanni, and promised to return to advise him in her capacity of consultant as soon as she had located Gloria. She couldn't imagine what topic she could give advice on that he didn't already have a firm opinion about. Madame Ambassador was giving out imperious commands.

No one seemed in evidence on the fourth floor, although the door to the backstairs stood open, so Margaret hastened to the office and the old desk. She opened the drawers and leafed again through the old papers and bills she'd found earlier.

It was very quiet upstairs, with only an occasional muffled thud or raised voice from below. The drawers held little of interest, now that she'd already found the chess piece.

Margaret closed all the drawers and stood up. As she did so she saw a shadow pass the door and she looked out cautiously. She caught a glimpse of Gloria entering the little hall that led to the small rooms at the back of the house. Hadn't someone, Gloria perhaps, mentioned an old sewing room and box rooms?

Gloria was wearing a peculiar, dreamy expression. Margaret was frankly surprised that she would come up to this floor with the recent attack still fresh and the old memories fresher still.

Before Margaret could call out to her, a very substantial-looking woman came huffing up the stairs.

"You're not Gloria Anton," the woman said challengingly, and Margaret admitted that she was not.

"She was just here. She went that way," Margaret informed her.

"I hope she doesn't think I'm going to climb four flights just to talk to her," the woman said. "I'm Penny Briggs. I do cozy nooks, leafy bowers, that sort of thing. The room she's given me is an awful little place on the ground floor. I thought I'd look about up here."

"I see," Margaret said. "I am Margaret Priam."

"I love snug little spaces where one can escape the cares of the streets and relax close to heaven. I hope there's a room up here with windows."

"I don't think this floor is being decorated," Margaret began, but Penny Briggs was lumbering heavily in the direction Gloria had taken. Margaret followed.

Penny Briggs flung open a door and said, "What nonsense is this?"

They found Gloria sitting on the floor of a storage room surrounded by old steamer trunks from which spilled faded gowns, a velvet cape, yellowing tennis clothes, jodhpurs, beaded evening bags.

Gloria was wrapped in a length of shimmering

emerald-green satin and was humming to herself as she rocked back and forth with her arms folded across her chest.

"Why, hello," Gloria said. "Penny dear, your room is on the first floor. I know you'll turn it into something sweet and pretty." Penny grimaced and proceeded down the hall, opening doors along the way.

Gloria seemed rather out of touch. Margaret wondered if she'd gotten into the vodka rather early today.

"Margaret, isn't this a beautiful color? Like a forest or a huge lawn. I remember seeing English lawns. Do your lawns at home look like this?" She stroked the green satin dreamily.

"Perhaps we ought to go downstairs," Margaret suggested, then she heard Penny shout, "Windows!"

"She must be in the sewing room," Gloria said wearily. "Tell her no, would you?"

"And then we'll go down," Margaret said.

"If we do, I'll tell you a secret," Gloria said. "You can't imagine what I found in Hannah's desk the other day."

"Something taped to the side of a drawer?"

Gloria pouted. "You peeked."

"No, I simply noticed the strips of tape, right after you'd been in there. What was it?"

"A joke," Gloria said. "A real joke. Eric was right."

"Come along." Margaret was tiring of Gloria and all the Gilpins.

Gloria stood unsteadily and swayed a bit. Margaret was rather more certain now that breakfast had been vodka and orange juice. "Peter didn't come home last night. I wonder where he could have been." Margaret took her arm and pointed her toward the door. Gloria was still swathed in the green satin, which trailed the floor behind her. Near the door to the office, Margaret left her for a moment to peer over the banister to see who on the floors below might be witness to Gloria's performance.

"Let's go down and see how the decorating boys and girls are coming," Gloria said. She flung aside the satin wrap, ran her hands through her hair and patted it into place, and proceeded down the stairs with dignity.

The third floor was bustling with activity. Eddie Leone was directing electricians, who were rewiring Juana de los Angeles's bedroom, while painters were laying a primer coat on the walls of the landing under the eye of the designer—unknown to Margaret—who was decorating the space.

"Eddie, what has become of my adorable husband?" Gloria inquired sweetly.

Eddie stopped his discussion with the electricians and turned to her. "Him and Centner are looking at some place in Jersey. They went out there last night, and said for me to pick them up this morning. We just got back."

"Now I know where my adorable husband was," Gloria continued in her sweet mode. "And here's my adorable brother."

"I got your message," Dougie said. "Pauline told me you said it was important."

"Pauline, poor Pauline. Dougie, you have been naughty."

"Look, Gloria, I'm really busy today. Tell me what this is about and let me get going downtown."

"Lady Margaret wants to talk with you," Gloria said.

He eyed Margaret. "Yeah? What about?"

"She's going to tell us who pushed our little brother down the stairs. Was it you, my much-married big brother?"

"What is all this?" Dougie was scowling.

"Nothing," Margaret told him. "I mean, Gloria asked me—"

"Stay out of our business," Dougie said. He turned to Gloria. "And you better go home and take a nap. You know, I understand better all the time why Leland dumped you. At least Angela knows how to behave in public."

"No, she doesn't." Gloria was furious. "And you don't know how to behave in public or private. I know all about you, Dougie. Hannah told me, and she'll tell everyone. But I will *not* pay for your silence, not anymore."

The decorators appeared to be trying to ignore the brother-sister argument, but were not succeeding. They were all at the doors to their rooms, listening to every word, and indeed, Margaret caught a glimpse of Giovanni and Bobby inching their way up the stairs from the floor below so as not to miss anything.

Suddenly, there was a tremendous crash from far below, and the sound of Godfrey Helms shouting. That broke the spell of Gloria and Dougie's argument, and everyone headed for the stairs and scrambled down to the first floor.

A deliveryman had dropped an enormous carton in the ground-floor foyer, toppling the ladder Alfred's boy had been using, although fortunately, it did not appear that he had been on it. The workmen stood about, apparently enjoying Godfrey's fit.

"Idiot!" Godfrey screamed. "If that's my chandelier . . ."

The dark-haired kitchen girl examined the box. "It's our range," she said, and shrugged. "It doesn't matter if it's broken, since we don't have to cook anything."

"You're not going to drag that thing through my dining room," Godfrey said. "The floors have just been finished. They're not dry yet. It will never get through the door anyhow."

"Maybe you'll have to get the construction guys to widen the door, then," the kitchen girl said.

"Not until I get my tools back," one of the workmen said. "Somebody stole a real good hammer." He glared at Godfrey.

"Well, I didn't steal your damned tools," Godfrey said, "and I'm not paying to change the door again. You should have brought the box in through the basement and up the elevator."

"Elevator's off-limits." Eddie had descended with the others. "Look, we'll handle it somehow." He was surprisingly soothing, and before long, everyone was calm and back to work.

"Giovanni, is there anything I can do?" Margaret asked, catching up with her new employer.

"Actually yes. I'm doing my room in shades of gray, something more modern than I usually do. I'll need you to run over to the Kistner Gallery to pick out some black-and-white photos and drawings. Fifties and sixties things. Gary Winogrand would be perfect. Maybe William Wegman's dogs. They're the right color. I want humor."

"I should think so, if everything is going to be gray,"

Margaret said, happy to have a useful task to attend to. "But don't we have enough dogs already?"

"Fay Ray and Battina are well-mannered photogenic weimaraners, quite unlike the flesh-and-blood animals Godfrey and Bobby are proposing. I'll want a little very careful color," Giovanni said. "Wait, I think Pace handles Wegman. Never mind, Kistner may have something. No English antiques this time. I want to stretch. Ask for Carl at the gallery. I've made all the arrangements for him to loan us what we want."

"I'll run over there this afternoon," Margaret said.

"You must have tea with me," Gloria interrupted. "Katya will be there. Now you can take Dougie off to one of the little rooms on the ground floor—is any furniture in any of them yet?—and see what he has to say for himself. Dougie! Don't you dare leave yet."

Chapter 14

*O*ne of the small rooms contained a couple of folding chairs. Dougie reluctantly sat, facing Margaret, only to be interrupted by Penny Briggs.

"My room," she said possessively. "No windows. But if that idiot Godfrey Helms can do faux windows . . ."

"We need a private moment, Penny," Margaret said, and turned to Dougie. "This is Gloria's idea. She seems to think I can discover what happened to Eric, even though it was so long ago, and I'm sure the police looked at everything very carefully."

"I told you that Eric found out some things about me that he was going to tell our mother and Grandfather," Dougie said. "I could have gotten around her, I always did. They used to say Eric was her favorite, but that's not so. She liked me the best, and Grandfather did, too. He thought I was going to step into his shoes when I got out of college. Well, he was gone by then, but I've done all right for myself."

Margaret remembered Gloria's claim that she'd loaned him money.

"Maybe you'd better tell me what Eric had found out."

"Look, I don't want to dig up all that stuff from the past. What good would it do?"

"Was it about you and Hannah?"

Dougie's jaw tightened. "Who told you that?"

"You mentioned something. And Hannah said . . . "

Now he stood up. "Have you been bothering her?"

"Why, no. I happened to run into her at the home of a friend."

"Poppy Dill." Dougie sounded disgusted. "Hannah said she was going to look her up. So I had a little fling with her. No big thing. So she was stealing the chessmen one by one. She took quite a few things. A little solid gold box that nobody ever noticed was missing. Hannah always liked money, never had enough. Eric threatened to tell Grandfather, because he found out everything, and Hannah would have ended up with nothing from him, but you can't imagine that she pushed Eric down the backstairs."

"I suppose you've kept in touch with her over the years. Even when she married Crouzat."

"Yeah, sort of." He suddenly seemed very uneasy.

"Ever send her money? I mean, has she asked for money?"

"What do you mean by that?"

"Merely curious. Let's suppose Hannah had knowledge that was worth money, which you say she likes. Say, if you and Hannah had your fling, and perhaps there was a child . . . There'd be a problem for you in the here and now. Pauline wouldn't like that, I think. Let's suppose Gloria figured all this out over the years, and has been threatening to share her suspicions."

"Bitches," Dougie muttered. "All of you. I have no children."

Margaret left Dougie then, to go about her business for Giovanni. When she left the house, Madame

Ambassador was directing the unloading of several large pieces of furniture from a van. "We'll just put it in the foyer," she was saying. "My room isn't ready to receive it. Alfred won't mind."

Margaret thought Alfred probably would mind, since she had just heard him discussing paint colors with Godfrey, to ensure that the entrance blended in with Godfrey's room.

"Damn the enfilade," Godfrey had been ranting. "I'm doing geranium walls, and I don't care what shade of fire-engine red you use. You'll look ridiculous, not me, so change *your* color. I'm not changing mine." She wasn't certain how the dispute had ended. Godfrey, after all, had a very large wolfhound on his team.

Now a couple of passersby stopped to watch the unloading, which Madame's supervision appeared to be hampering.

"Do not damage that piece. It's very valuable." She turned to the watching men. "These people cannot be trusted, they have no appreciation of fine—be careful, I said!" She raised her hand to her brow in exasperation and her formidable bosom heaved a deep sigh.

The two spectators exchanged wry glances and started to stroll slowly down the street toward Central Park. Meanwhile Madame followed the deliverymen, who were gingerly carrying a delicate daybed upholstered in pale yellow up the stairs into the house. Margaret had another thought and went back into the house. Most of the decorators were busy in their rooms, so the more public spaces were empty. Madame's voice could be heard above, giving further firm instructions. Giovanni was standing in the doorway of the old music room, surveying it pensively.

"I wanted to ask," Margaret said, "about the framing and matting and so forth. Or do you want to see the photos first?"

"You handle it," Giovanni told her. "Black matting, I think, and narrow matte silver frames, a mix of horizontal and vertical. Carl will take care of the framing. You know, I may turn this back into a music room, but it's hell to move in a baby grand."

"What about an upright? Or a player piano."

He threw up his hands. "Let it be a sitting room, with plenty of audiovisual stuff to dazzle the visitors. I say, Margaret, is Gloria all right? She seemed quite . . . feverish."

"Something upset her. Again. Is she still around?"

Giovanni shrugged. "I saw her talking to Dougie, a rather heated discussion. Then I came back up here, and I think maybe I saw her going on up to the next floor, but I'm not certain. Hey!" He cocked his head and listened. "I thought the elevator was out of service."

Margaret heard the hum of the ascending elevator. "It was." It didn't stop at the second floor but continued upward. "It's probably Eddie. He seems to like to ride the elevator." But then Eddie emerged from the library with a pained expression, as though he had been bested by Bobby Henley.

"I'm going to find Gloria," Margaret said. "She doesn't need to spend every moment at the house, does she?"

"She has some decisions to make, but not urgently. We designers know our business," Giovanni said.

"Although if I hear one more time about Helms's damned door or dog, I may scream. Eddie will watch over us closely. Send her home."

Juana de los Angeles was in her third-floor bedroom, sketching rapidly. Margaret glimpsed a canopied bed at the center of the sketch.

"Ah, Lady Margaret . . . This room is in pretty good shape, all I have to do is have the walls painted and lay down the carpeting."

"Have you seen Gloria?"

"What? Oh, no. Not for hours. Two slipper chairs, I think, near the windows. And a lovely big dressing table with lots of mirrors. I wish there was more light. . . ."

Margaret withdrew and started up to the fourth floor.

Suddenly there was a disturbance above, out of her view, a loud thump and an almost simultaneous scream. The clang of the elevator door and the hum of the elevator descending. Margaret raced up the stairs.

The door to the backstairs stood open, and the end of the length of green satin that Gloria had draped herself in earlier was on the floor just outside the door. The rest of the fabric appeared to cascade down the stairs.

"Gloria!" Margaret scrambled toward the open door.

Juana stode up the stairs from her room. "What is the matter?" she asked breathlessly.

Margaret peered down the dim stairway, then said over her shoulder, "Go down the other staircase to the second floor and find Eddie Leone, or Giovanni or Bobby. Anybody. Quickly!"

Juana moved quickly. Margaret could hear her calling out shrilly as she herself carefully walked down the narrow, dark stairs, steadying herself with her hands on the walls on either side. There were no lights on the stairs, and she tried to avoid stepping on the slippery satin to keep from tumbling headfirst into the darkness. At the landing of what would be the third floor, she found Gloria, crumpled in a heap, moaning softly. She was alarmed to see blood seeping into Gloria's blond coiffure as she knelt beside her. Suddenly the door to the stairs from the third-floor landing was flung open and Eddie Leone's form filled the space.

"What happened?"

"Gloria fell," Margaret answered. "Or she was pushed. She might have struck her head—look at all this blood."

"Hey, you!" Eddie called to someone out on the landing. "Yeah, you, whatever your name is." He pulled a cellular phone from his jacket pocket and handed it back to someone. "Call 9-1-1. Now. Mrs. Anton's been hurt. We need a doc and an ambulance."

"I don't think you should move her," Margaret said as Eddie appeared to be about to lift her up. "I mean, something could be broken, a concussion. . . ."

"Yeah, a lot of blood," Eddie said. "She musta hit her head. What's that?" He pointed up the stairs at the piece of satin.

"Some cloth Gloria found in one of the storage rooms," Margaret said. "Slippery underfoot." She was trying to feel for a pulse, but since Gloria continued to moan, she was obviously still alive. Suddenly there was a considerable hubbub outside on the landing as the decorators gathered, summoned by Juana.

"Keep them away," Margaret called, but Bobby broke through and was suddenly kneeling beside her.

"Darling, are you all right?" He looked accusingly at Margaret. "How did this happen?"

"I don't know, Bobby, but I think you ought to—wait. I heard the elevator, just as I was reaching the fourth floor. It was going down. Eddie, who is in the house who might dare to use the elevator?"

"Me," he said, "but I didn't have nothing to do with this—"

"Bobby, stay here with Gloria, but don't try to move her. The emergency medical people should be here soon. And we ought to have the police. Come on, Eddie, we're going to the basement."

Apparently whatever Margaret wanted from Eddie, she got. He followed her out onto the landing, where Godfrey, Juana, Penny, the kitchen girls, Alfred—indeed, everyone except Madame Ambassador—stood around looking frightened or interested.

"The main stairs," Margaret said. "Lead the way."

"Do we really need the cops?" He seemed uneasy about that.

"Definitely. I'm almost certain she was hit and then pushed."

On the ground floor, the trompe l'oeil lady was cowering in the doorway to her room. "Is everything all right?" she asked timidly as Margaret and Eddie passed her. Margaret stopped.

"There's been an accident. Have you seen Dougie Gilpin?"

"I don't think so," the woman said, "but I don't know him, so I couldn't say for sure."

Margaret heard a siren outside. "Eddie, let the ambulance people in, and the police, if they've come, and show them upstairs to Gloria."

She'd have to cross the still-tacky floor of Godfrey's dining room to get to the back of the house and the stairs down to the basement. Then she saw that a pathway of planks on two-by-fours had been laid around the left side of the room to the door to the new kitchen area, to allow passage without walking on the actual floor. As she carefully made her way around the room, she heard Eddie's voice behind her saying, "Hey, boss. Am I glad to see you."

Boss? Peter Anton had arrived just in time to be with his injured wife. Margaret was not thinking clearly. Her intent was to get to the basement to see if the elevator had gone there. It had not been on the third floor when she emerged from the backstairs, she wasn't sure about the second floor, but it was not on the ground floor when she and Eddie got there.

She found the stairs and walked down into the old basement. There were plenty of lights on, even in the old-fashioned kitchen, and in the billiards room, where she was not surprised to see Dougie knocking a few balls around a high pool table.

"Dougie, has anyone come down here in the elevator in the last few minutes?"

Dougie looked up, puzzled. "Elevator isn't supposed to be used," he said. "Anyhow, I just came down here a few minutes ago myself. I don't have time to talk now. Pauline's picking me up. She's probably waiting outside in a cab right now. What's up?"

"Gloria took a bad tumble on the backstairs. History repeating itself. We've already discussed what she knows, and what I suspect. And now someone's trying to silence her."

Dougie looked at her briefly, expressionless. "No kidding?" was all he said as he made a nice bank shot.

"Is there any way in or out of the basement? Other than the way I came, I mean."

"Sure. There's a door that leads to this little alley kind of thing out to the street so the tradesmen in the old days could make deliveries without tramping through the house. In my great-grandfather's day, the iceman used to deliver ice, and the coal man brought in coal, and the servants used it. It's been locked and bolted for decades. It's never used now, although they'll probably have to open it up so that these decorator people can move all their stuff in without tripping over each other." He finally put down his cue. "Say, is Gloria okay?"

"I wondered when you'd ask," Margaret said.

"Geez, if she were dead, you would have said something right off, wouldn't you? What I meant was, is it serious? Should I do something?"

"I think it's being handled. Apparently her husband arrived just as the ambulance people did."

"Lot of help he'll be. He's probably praying for her to die so he can inherit. . . ."

Margaret remembered Gloria announcing how rich she was, and thought, Well, if it wasn't a simple accident, Peter Anton was immediately suspect, but how could he have gotten to the fourth floor, slipped away, and then walked in the front door?

Except that as the current owner of this house, he, along with his partner, would surely be aware of the back door to the alley. He would be aware of the elevator, and the layout of the place. But so would Dougie, for that matter. And even Hannah.

"Where's that door?" Margaret asked. "I want a look at it."

The door, when Dougie showed it to her, did not look as though it had been unopened for decades. A new lock had been installed, and the dust of years had been recently swept into a pile to one side. The elevator, she noted, had come to rest on the basement level.

"So you saw no one suspicious or unexpected here?"

Dougie shook his head, but Margaret didn't put much stock in his allegiance to the truth.

"We'd better find out how Gloria is doing," Margaret said. "I hope she's well enough to tell me what she was doing back up on the fourth floor."

Gloria had been taken away, and Eddie was about to leave with a man Margaret assumed was Peter Anton. Then he turned, and with a shock, she recognized him as one of the two men who had been watching the unloading of Madame Ambassador's furniture outside the house, shortly before Gloria fell.

Chapter 15

Bobby Henley was sitting on the stairs looking dejected.

"She broke something—an arm, an ankle. One of the EMS guys said maybe there's a concussion." He looked at Margaret mournfully. "She looked awful. Do you think someone actually hit her?" He didn't seem to expect an answer, but sighed and continued, "I hate it when bad things happen to good friends. Margaret, I think Gloria is going to die."

"That was her attacker's intention. Where is everybody now?"

"They took off pretty fast," Bobby said, "when someone mentioned that the police would be called in. Margaret, she kept muttering that it was an accident, and she wasn't going to tell. Tell what?"

"Tell who tried to murder her. Now we may never know."

"Margaret, where are you going?"

"Nosy people lose their noses," she said. "I'm going back to the fourth floor. It wasn't an accident."

Bobby scrambled to his feet. "I'm coming with you."

"Shhh," Margaret said quickly. "Don't say anything more." Dougie had emerged from his basement lair.

"What's the story?" Dougie did not seem to be particularly concerned about his sister's fate.

"She broke her arm," Margaret answered. "Nothing serious. She claims she slipped on some fabric that had been left on the floor and just toppled down the stairs. Maybe we should consider keeping the doors to those stairs locked. We can't have visitors to the showhouse disappearing down the backstairs and subsequently bringing lawsuits against us. She might have been struck. There was a lot of blood."

"What rot," Dougie scoffed. "She's imagining things. She's always been too damned imaginative. And nobody's going to get lost in this place. Pete'll see to that."

"If anyone does get lost in the house," Margaret said, "we'll get the monks to pray for their safe return." She momentarily flashed on a picture of a row of brown-cowled monks at a long, highly polished dining table looking perfectly divine against the backdrop of Godfrey's lovely geranium walls and faux window with its artfully concealed sunset lighting. The wolfhound tossed the bone he was gnawing into the rushes on the floor. It was all too much like the tales Margaret remembered from childhood about the olden days when Priam's Priory housed a religious community, and the brothers dined by candlelight in the great hall.

Dougie looked at his watch. "I should be catching up with my wife before she bankrupts me. You people are too much."

"*He* is too much," Bobby commented as Dougie strolled out the front door. "I never could figure out why he's as successful as people say he is. I guess Pauline makes up for his deficiencies."

Margaret quickly changed the subject. "You didn't see Angela Forsythe around here today, did you?"

"You mean, the one person who has it in for—As a matter of fact, I did. Look, I don't want to get Angela in trouble, but she and what's her name?—Terry Thompson—stopped in a while ago. Terry was after me and the rest of the designers to get the artwork and copy for the showhouse journal to her. You know, the sketches of our rooms, and the list of sources for the furnishings. Then she leaned on us a bit to buy ads in the book. Angela seemed to be acting as her obedient assistant, quiet for a change, especially after yesterday. How long they were here, I don't know." He looked at Margaret solemnly. "They might have gone all the way up to the fourth floor, for all I know. Maybe Pauline Gilpin could tell you. She was hanging about with Alfred on the first floor, but I saw her leaving right after the ambulance came."

"Let's go upstairs," Margaret suggested. "I want a look at that storage room on the fourth floor."

The house was eerily quiet now that nearly everyone was gone. A couple of painters were still working in Madame's room, where the furniture was protected with the old sheets, and in Giovanni's room, which was becoming as gray as a thundercloud. Bobby's wood refinishers had departed, leaving only the heavy odor of chemicals.

"What are we looking for?" Bobby asked. The green satin was still on the fourth-floor landing. He followed Margaret down the hallway to the box room, where the contents of the steamer trunks were still spilling out.

"I'm not sure," Margaret confessed. "I'll know when I see it."

Bobby began inspecting the clothes. "Look at these fabulous old things," he exclaimed. "The vintage clothing people would kill to have this stuff." He held up a short beaded dress. "Flapper era, worth a fortune. Oooh! Look at this, will you?" He had pulled back a drape to reveal an iron rod from which were hanging tulle ball gowns in plastic bags. "They should be stored in acid-free paper," he said severely, then added shamefacedly, "but I guess that's not the most important thing right now. Gloria told me nobody ever bothered to clear out the upper floors. She used to play dress-up here."

Margaret started to rummage through the steamer trunks, pulling out drawers and sorting through stiff leather handbags, piles of embroidered handkerchiefs, gauzy scarves, and worn deck shoes. Finally, she pulled out a yellowed envelope with masking tape still adhering to the edges. "What is important," she said, "could be this." She lifted the flap and removed a sheet of paper, unfolded it, and read.

"Aha." She refolded the page and put it into her handbag. "Much clearer now, Bobby. Gloria has been busy. But why on earth would she leave this here where anyone might find it?"

"Explain," Bobby said. "This has got to be really exciting dish. That paper looked like a photostat, not a Xerox copy. People had photostats made of important documents before Mr. Xerox invaded our lives, so it's some years old."

Margaret was still rummaging. Suddenly she stopped and pulled her hand from the drawer. She peered in, then, using a silk scarf, carefully removed a heavy hammer with a scarred wooden handle.

"Do you suppose it's the construction guy's missing hammer?" she said. "Probably. I guess . . . It really is a police matter now." She put the hammer back in the drawer, perplexed about what her next step should be. "Let's go elsewhere, Bobby. The atmosphere here is too oppressive. I have to assume that my tea with Gloria this afternoon has been canceled, although I would have liked to talk to the old servant. We'll call later to see how Gloria's doing."

They left the house, where distant noises suggested that Godfrey had found a new occasion to berate a workman, and walked over to Madison Avenue and up a couple of blocks to a coffee shop not far from Hunter College.

"Spill it," Bobby said eagerly. "What's the paper about? And did someone use that hammer to whack Gloria?"

Margaret gazed at Bobby. She did not know him well, but Gloria trusted him, and he was clearly devoted to her. So she said, "The photostat put Gloria in a rather dangerous position, assuming someone didn't want her to share it. Look, I think I should call my policeman friend about all this."

Bobby sighed and ordered coffee from the elderly Greek waiter. "You're going to go all mysterious on me," he said.

"Not really. Tuna on a roll," she told the waiter. "I'm starved. I didn't get lunch, although I'm scheduled for a take-out Chinese feast tonight." She thought briefly of De Vere, of De Vere's first wife, of the hypothetical woman he might now be seeing. She didn't rel-

ish calling him to mention the hammer, she realized as
she searched her handbag for money for the pay phone.
The hammer was hidden, so maybe she would wait
until tonight to tell him. If Gloria was all right, there
was no point in stirring up trouble.

"What is it that Gloria knows?" Bobby was pleading.

"Have you ever considered marriage?" Margaret
asked, then added quickly, "Probably not."

"I look dreadful in white," Bobby said. "And you're
right. It's never crossed my mind."

"What I mean is, if you—one considers marriage, it
should be in terms of a serious commitment. Long-
term, and never mind how easy divorce has become.
There are all sorts of other concerns—the couple's
families, the future, compatibility, where you'll live,
what sort of work you'll do, the class you come from
and what you're accustomed to in terms of lifestyle. . . ." She could have been reciting her own concerns about De Vere.

Bobby shrugged. "What has this to do with Gloria?
She and Peter seem quite satisfied with their lives,
happy with each other, although his history doesn't appear to match Gloria's in any of the areas you mentioned. I mean, the Gilpins . . ."

Margaret bit into her tuna sandwich. "There are
other Gilpins besides Gloria."

"Dougie?" Bobby was surprised. "His wife is nice
enough."

"But is she his wife?"

"Whatever do you mean? Of course she is. I remember when Dougie and Pauline got married; it was just
after he divorced his first wife, Dorothy. One sees her

around occasionally still. She's very anti-Dougie, now that I think of it."

Margaret looked at Bobby seriously, before she spoke. "Bobby, do you really want to help figure out who harmed Gloria? Can I trust you to keep secrets?"

"Need you ask? Gloria is about the best friend I have." He looked so concerned, Margaret decided to tell him what she knew.

"The thing is, there was yet another wife, long ago, as that paper I found proves. When Dougie was a college boy he was enamored of old Douglas Gilpin's secretary, Hannah Garber. The family had big plans for Dougie: a very socially prominent bride, stepping into Douglas Gilpin's business shoes. But the younger brother Eric was always spying on his siblings."

"He found out that Dougie had gotten married to the old man's secretary? It's a minor blot on the family escutcheon, but no big thing."

"It might be a big thing if the first Mrs. Dougie made it an issue. She's close to Poppy Dill, who could spread the tale, especially if Gloria is involved. The brother's death, the mother's suicide, and now her accident . . . and Dougie's marital woes."

"Well, Pauline would hate to be mixed up in that sort of gossip and scandal," Bobby said. "She's quite proper." He leaned forward. "But who else knows or cares? We don't."

"Hannah could put both Dougie and Pauline in a rather difficult position. Hannah also has a history of blackmail. And there's the matter of Eric's death. She was present, but I think Dougie the more likely perpetrator."

"Then she's really got something to blackmail him

with." Bobby's excitement seemed a bit inappropriate, under the circumstances. "So Dougie murdered the brother to silence him about the marriage, and now he tried to murder Gloria to maintain that silence. Did Gloria know about the marriage and the murder?"

"I think she did. She told me she'd seen Hannah. She could have found out then. Gloria has a way of getting things from people, even if they don't want to surrender."

"Well, Dougie didn't succeed in finishing off Gloria," Bobby said.

"Not yet," Margaret said, "but I don't know how to prove it, or protect her without making it all public."

"I suppose we could enlist Peter Anton's aid in protecting Gloria from her brother."

"The thing is," Margaret said, "I . . . I have my suspicions about him as well." She told Bobby about seeing him on the street, about the back way into the mansion, the elevator just before Gloria fell, and Peter's appearance at the front door. "There's a money thing going on," she said. "Gloria seems to be bankrolling Anton and his partner. She told me she was very rich."

"I'm not a terrific fan of Anton's," Bobby said, "but there are a lot of rich wives and not-so-rich husbands, and you don't see the wives getting killed off regularly. It's too risky. The police always suspect the husband first, and with her money . . ."

"There's always Angela," Margaret said. "No love lost there."

"And she was at the house today. Although I don't imagine she knows her way about the place. Well, we have quite a lineup of suspects, only no one's been murdered."

"Maybe we'll have to arrange something," Margaret said.

"What 'we' are you talking about?" Bobby said.

"I meant, we—you and I—will have to draw out the villain of the piece. I know pretty much everything. We owe it to Gloria."

"I owe her a lot," Bobby said slowly, "and I'll help if I can, but . . . Archer would kill *me* if I get damaged. What about the other woman? The secretary?"

"She's leaving the city tomorrow, I think. She certainly knows the house, but I don't see her risking the loss of Dougie's financial support. Maybe we should go back to the house. You probably have a lot to do, and it should be pretty quiet and empty by now."

"Speaking of an empty house," Bobby began, and told her about hearing the elevator the night he'd been there alone.

"A lot of traffic for an empty house," Margaret said. "I guess we'll have to find out from Gloria what happened today. Maybe she saw someone or knows who hit her or pushed her."

"Maybe she simply fell," Bobby said. "I don't like the idea of murder."

"Nor do I," Margaret said. "But if the right person knows that I know what Gloria knows . . ."

"You, too, could end up damaged. I wouldn't much like that either."

"I ought to go to the gallery and pick out Giovanni's photos before I can't manage it. And I think I will drop in at Gloria's place, because even if she's not been released from the hospital, the old servant Katya is supposed to be at the d'Este and I'd like to talk to her. She was there when Eric died."

"If you're going first to Gloria, I'd like to come with you."

"I think not," Margaret said. "If we get into the matter of Dougie, the fewer people who know you know the better. And if Gloria knows, she might say something to Peter or Dougie, or—"

"All right, I understand. I think I'll run around to all my fabric sources and then to the International Kennel Club about the golden retriever."

"They have mostly puppies," Margaret said. "Surely you're not going to inflict the showhouse on a puppy, or vice versa. Look up people who have trained animals for hire. I think that's what Godfrey intends to do about the wolfhound."

Bobby looked crestfallen. "I hate it when Godfrey is a step ahead of me."

They parted on Madison, with Bobby heading back to the house and Margaret catching a cab to the Villa d'Este hotel.

Margaret spoke on the house phone to the accented woman she thought was probably Katya. Gloria had not yet been released by the hospital. There was no other news. Margaret remembered her last glimpse of Gloria and did not view the outcome optimistically.

"May I come up and speak with you, Katya?" she asked.

There was a pause. "I am not sure if Madame permits . . ."

"Mrs. Anton invited me to tea this afternoon to meet you. She has asked me to examine the matter of her brother's death, and since you were there at the time . . ." She took Katya's silence as assent, went to the elevator, and rode it to the twelfth floor. A short, squarish woman, very old, answered her ring. Katya looked exactly like photographs of Russian peasant women Margaret had seen in books about the old Russian empire. A grandmother with thinning white hair and a myriad of wrinkles around her pale blue eyes.

"Please to sit down," she said, and directed Margaret to the white sofa. "I bring tea now."

She served tea in a glass in the Russian fashion, and there was an array of small cakes and biscuits on very lovely china plates. Holding her own glass of tea, Katya perched on the edge of a chair. "You are wishing to ask something?"

Margaret thought. What did she wish to ask Katya? Well, she could make a stab. "Do you know who murdered young Eric?"

"No murder!" Katya was indignant. "Is falling on stairs. Very dangerous."

"Yet the same thing has happened to Mrs. Anton. Doesn't this worry you?"

"Worry yes, because Miss Gloria is falling also." Her eyes darted back and forth as though she feared someone was lurking about, eavesdropping.

"There's no one to hear, Katya. Think back to the old days." Goodness knew how old Katya was now, if the old days were forty years in the past, and before that, her years in Russia.

Katya closed her eyes. "Eric is dying in my arms. I am weeping. Boris is shouting, and running. I hear Miss Gloria calling from upstairs and Mr. Dougie saying to her to stop from coming down."

"Is Eric saying anything?"

Katya's face looked as though a steel door had shut on it. "He is saying nothing, but he is holding a little figure tight, tight in his hand. The queen from the chess set. I am giving it to the policeman when he comes." Katya was silent again, but she appeared to be considering whether to speak further. "Is something else in his hand. I do not give to police. A bad thing for the family if I show it. I show to you, you will know what to do." She reached into the pocket of the heavy cardigan sweater she wore, even though the suite was quite warm, and the tea had been scalding. "I am taking this from the little locked box when Madame is saying you would come today." She handed Margaret a white handkerchief wrapped around a folded sheet of paper, much handled, with dark marks along the folds as though it had been opened and closed many times.

The paper was flimsy with age, and Margaret opened it carefully. There were small tears at the folds and the print of the photostat was faded in places. A duplicate of what Margaret had found on the fourth floor.

"Do you know what this is?" Margaret asked.

Katya nodded. "The wicked Miss Hannah who is always touching and looking at Mr. Dougie. She is thinking I do not see, but I see everything. And how much older was she? He was a boy in his heart, but a man in other ways. There is a child to come, she is telling him, and I hear. I am in my rooms up there, praying to the saints, and she does not know that I hear. She cries and she says they will go to the government office and they will marry. He is frightened, but she has put a spell on him, and he is believing her. They get the paper that says they are married, but he cannot say this to his mother or his grandfather, but Eric learns of this, and . . ." She shook her head. "He was like that, he is wishing for . . . for praise for finding about things. Again I am praying in my room, and he is saying to Dougie and Miss Hannah what he knows is true. Dougie is saying he will regret telling the grandfather and the mother. I fear for what will happen. But there is no child to come. I know this, too. Then Miss Hannah comes to Mr. Gilpin and tells her she is going away with a man she will marry. It is not Mr. Dougie, another man."

"René Crouzat?" Margaret asked.

"I do not know this, but I think, how can this be? But I do not see the paper saying they are married until Eric is dying in my arms. But I am thinking is a good thing if she leaves with this other man, but Eric is knowing all about his brother and Miss Hannah. He is still saying he will tell the grandfather. Then I am in my kitchen preparing the food for Miss Gloria's last meal at the house, and I am suddenly hearing the boy falling on the stairs. Dougie comes from the elevator, I do not forget his smiling. He is saying . . ."

Again Katya closed her eyes and was silent. Margaret waited.

"Is saying the boy will tell no more jokes. We have stopped the jokes."

"So it was Dougie and Hannah who pushed him?"

Katya's anguished expression gave her the answer.

"When I find the paper, I do not tell Dougie. What does an old woman know of these things? I keep it safe, for many years. He does not know I have it."

"He will soon know that I have it," Margaret said.

Katya reached out to grab the paper from her, but Margaret, rather unkindly, kept it from her reach. "It's not safe for you to keep it."

Katya said, "The woman, Miss Hannah, does not know. When I see her looking so proud and she is now not young . . ."

"You've seen her? Where?"

"Here in this room. She is eating dinner with Miss Gloria. She is staying here at this hotel. I look in when I hear the angry words."

"What words?"

"About the law, about money. About Eric. I do not understand. Miss Gloria is saying that Dougie, the family, will not allow her to say such things, and that woman is saying, 'When I say to the police what Dougie did, you will not speak to me this way.' "

The telephone rang suddenly in the quiet room. Katya hobbled over to answer it. She really was very old. She murmured quietly so that Margaret could not hear, but all at once she uttered a terrible shriek, dropped the phone, and sank to the floor. Margaret rushed to her and picked up the phone.

"Lady Margaret Priam here. Is there a problem?" Katya appeared to have fainted, but happily her eyelids fluttered open.

"This is Peter Anton. We haven't met, but I know your name from . . . from Gloria." His voice was breaking now. "She died. She didn't even make it to the hospital. The Emergency Medical Service guy said she'd been slammed pretty hard." Peter Anton sounded genuinely grief-stricken. "I . . . I wanted Katya to call Christine."

"Katya has fainted."

"Could you call . . . ?"

Margaret could, albeit unwillingly, because she wasn't sure how to tell the young woman that her mother had been murdered.

Chapter 16

Christine did not take the news well, but she promised to try to locate her brother Ricky somewhere in Asia. She also agreed to inform her father. "I'll ask him to call Granddad in Florida. I . . . I couldn't do it, or tell Uncle Dougie."

"I will call your uncle Dougie," Margaret said, "unless Peter has already done so."

Poppy Dill, who needed to know everything before anyone else, was grateful that Margaret called her, and immediately asked who would take over the showhouse.

"Surely it can't go on," Margaret said, remembering that Gloria had named her second in command.

"Surely it must," Poppy insisted. "The SPDA is expecting to have it, and it will be a lovely memorial to Gloria."

"Gloria isn't in need of memorials," Margaret said. "She's more in need of justice. Someone did this to her."

"The police will figure it out," Poppy said. "You're right. You shouldn't be doing their dirty work."

Although Margaret had never said such a thing, she winced at the thought of the police. But of course, in the case of a death like this one . . . She remembered the hammer hidden on the fourth floor. The weapon, surely.

"The showhouse," Poppy repeated. "Peter Anton will want to have it go on, I'm sure. It will be such a selling point for the house when it goes on the market. You'd be perfect, but if you won't do it, you'll have to think of someone."

Margaret smiled briefly as she hung up. There was always Angela, and better yet, there was Terry Thompson, who was never reluctant to take on mighty challenges. Of course, if Terry chaired the event, Angela was sure to be involved, but now that Gloria was gone, it didn't matter so much.

"May I speak with Mr. Gilpin? Lady Margaret Priam here."

"It's Pauline, Lady Margaret. I'm afraid Dougie is out. Can I assist?"

"Gloria died from injuries suffered in her fall today at her grandfather's house. Perhaps you would be kind enough to inform Dougie."

"How awful," Pauline said. "Gloria gone. I . . . I can't believe it. . . . Is there anything else?"

Margaret bit her lip and took a deep breath. "You might tell him that I know everything, with the help of Katya and Gloria."

"I see," Pauline said. "Everything, you say? I don't understand."

"He will understand," Margaret said. Though she herself didn't quite understand, she was convinced that Dougie had committed murder, and had calmly gone down in the elevator to chalk up a billiard cue and knock a few balls around the table as his sister lay on her green satin vision of an English lawn.

The last call was to Terry Thompson, who was unashamedly delighted at the prospect of chairing the showhouse committee. "At least Gloria didn't wait to die until the program and journal were all printed with her name in them," Terry said, "although I am sorry to hear the news. I can handle the house easily. I suppose I'll have to get the okay of the SPDA, but what can they say? The decorators have been flinging themselves into their work, so all I'll have to do is moderate disputes and see that a lot of people buy tickets to the gala and show up to tour the house." She hesitated. "Peter Anton won't snatch the place out from under our feet, will he?"

"The feeling seems to be that a grand showhouse will be profitable for him and Richard Centner when they get around to selling the place. I shouldn't worry. But," she added, "if he asks for a fee, I'd just pay it." Margaret didn't think Peter had killed his wife over a user's fee, but one never knew about these people.

"Hate to say it," Terry said, "but the publicity won't hurt us. Do you think Poppy Dill would write something?"

"I find it hard to predict what Poppy will do," Margaret said. "I'll see that you get any showhouse material that Gloria had."

Finally that part was over. Margaret felt she ought to go around to the house and let the decorators know that all would continue as planned. Then she'd go to the gallery for Giovanni's pictures.

Eddie was sitting in the foyer, looking dejected, when she arrived. Even the sight of Lady Margaret failed to bring a smile to his face.

"I don't know what to say," he said. "She was okay, you know, easy to work for. It had to happen, though. . . ."

"Why do you say that?"

"Too much booze. It runs in the family, the boss says. She lost her footing or something."

"Or something. Do the designers know she died?"

"I didn't tell 'em. You know, I keep from speaking direct to them every chance I get."

"Then I'll have to tell them."

She went to the dining room, where Godfrey had made major progress. The floor was dry. Part of one wall had been painted a rosy geranium. Molding was in place for the faux window, and a bolt of drapery material leaned against the wall next to it. An electrician was finishing the wiring for the chandelier, while the long table was pushed to the side and at least a dozen chairs were stacked in a corner. Godfrey stood near the door to the kitchen, chin in hand. The other hand held a lead to the largest dog Margaret had ever seen, square-headed, long-legged, and about the size of a small pony as it sprawled on a rather attractive Oriental rug in shades of red, pale yellow, and yes, geranium. The dog raised its head as Margaret approached, then thumped it back down on the carpet, perhaps feeling that it wouldn't be noticed—an impossibility, given its size—and its nap continued undisturbed.

"Godfrey, have you heard? Gloria died in hospital."

Godfrey opened his eyes very wide and his mouth dropped open. "From that silly fall? I can't believe it. Say, Angela was at the house today. Did she . . . ?"

"I think not," Margaret said, "but I also think it was not a simple accident."

"You and I were here, you went upstairs. . . ."

"And I reached the fourth floor just when she took the tumble. I have to find Bobby. They were so close."

"Mind that dog he's gotten. It nearly attacked poor Daisy here." Daisy opened an eye at the sound of her name. Margaret tried to imagine any dog with the courage to attack an Irish wolfhound. She remembered the stirring sight of four or five wolfhounds loping across the green fields of an estate a friend owned not too far from Dublin. Unfortunately, she was told, wolves had pretty much disappeared from Ireland, and the hounds didn't get the sport they once did.

Bobby was in his library sitting in a big, comfortable leather chair. A benign-looking golden retriever sat at his feet with its head on his knee, gazing adoringly at him.

"I heard," was the first thing he said. He was barely holding back his tears. "Who did it? Dougie? Anton?"

"We don't know anyone 'did' it," Margaret said.

"You found a hammer where hammers don't live. That sounds to me like someone did something."

"I've left some bait, so maybe we'll catch a rat."

"Maybe that awful hound Godfrey found will catch the rat. It's not like my beautiful princess." Bobby spoke to the dog, which thumped its tail enthusiastically. "I dropped by the kennel place after I left you, and we fell instantly in love. I think I'll call her Marilyn, although she's not quite the same sort of blond."

"Don't get too attached," Margaret warned. "The showhouse only lasts two weeks."

"Archer will adore her. I plan to keep her, unless Godfrey's beast devours her."

"I understand that Irish wolfhounds are not vicious,

although like the proverbial eight-hundred-pound go-
rilla, they do pretty much what they want."

Margaret made her way from room to room, telling
her sad news to the decorators, all of whom wanted to
be reassured that the project would proceed as
planned, after all the work they'd done in the past
week. Finally she fled to the fourth floor, where there
was no one to be seen. Margaret settled herself in the
storage room, sat on a pile of old tennis sweaters, and
leaned against a trunk.

She took out the paper she'd received from Katya. It
was definitely a photostat of a marriage certificate is-
sued by the state of New York, signifying that Douglas
Gilpin IV, student, and Hannah Garber, spinster, had
been married by a justice of the peace some thirty-
eight years before. Eric had died clutching the paper in
his hand. It was the same document she'd found here
in this room, where Gloria had hidden it.

According to Katya's eavesdropping, Hannah had
coerced Dougie into the marriage by telling him that
she was pregnant . . . but if Katya was to be believed—
and Margaret was inclined to believe her—she wasn't
expecting anything except a share of the Gilpin
fortune.

Both Eric years ago and Gloria more recently had
learned of the marriage. Both of them were dead.

What did it matter now? Unless there was something more.

Margaret was on her feet and again rummaging
through the trunks. She opened the old handbags and
pulled out the low drawers meant for gloves and stock-
ings. She opened the drawer where she had found the
hammer. If it was the murder weapon, she didn't want

the murderer to come back looking for it. She wrapped it in an old chemise, being careful not to touch the handle or the head, and went to Hannah's office.

The house below seemed very quiet now, the decorators perhaps having gone away to console themselves over Gloria's death. They had taken it surprisingly hard, especially Bobby.

Looking through the desk again would yield nothing, she was sure, so she placed the hammer in the drawer with the masking tape on the side. The murderer would have to search the floor to retrieve it. Then she sat on the floor with her back against the wall and thought about what to do next.

She heard the elevator. Again. Who could be doing this constant riding up and down?

Margaret waited. She heard the inner door of the elevator slide open and then the outer grille, but no one appeared and there was no sound outside the office. On her hands and knees, Margaret crept to the door and peered out. On the dimly lighted landing, she saw a figure wrapped in a long dark coat, wearing a fedora-like hat, the face covered by a swathe of net veil. It seemed to her that it was not a man but a woman.

The person must have heard Margaret creeping back into the office, because she—if it was a woman— turned sharply and looked toward the door.

Margaret stood up, relieved that it was not Dougie or Peter Anton. For a moment she almost thought she knew who it was. But it was so unlikely, she hesitated. The house was full of people who probably had no business here, but if this was Gloria's murderer, she ought to offer a challenge.

"What are you doing here?" the person asked, edging slowly in Margaret's direction.

"I might ask the same of you," Margaret said. "There's nothing left to find here. The hammer is hidden. I almost understand why Gloria died."

"Do you indeed? I don't think so."

"But I will," Margaret said.

"Ah . . ." Suddenly the person lunged across the short space between them, catching Margaret by surprise. She felt powerful hands around her neck, although they were not sufficiently strong to incapacitate her. Margaret shoved with all her might and the person released the hold on her neck, then stumbled quickly toward the elevator as Margaret lost her balance and fell to her knees. By the time Margaret had gotten to her feet, taken a breath, and regained her composure, the elevator was beginning its descent. She did not think she could take the stairs fast enough to catch it. It would probably go to the basement, and who knew what barriers lay between the fourth floor and there? An Irish wolfhound at the very least.

She wondered if the hammer was safe left here in the desk. On the other hand, she didn't care to wander through the house with it. Margaret looked around. There was no less obvious and more secure hiding place than the drawer, but the murderer could so easily return and retrieve it as Margaret was going downstairs.

Then she had a thought. She descended hastily, to the floor below, and found Kenneth's room—newly painted blue, with, as predicted, the start of a white-stenciled flowery border along the top near the ceiling. Several covered wicker baskets were piled in a corner.

Margaret took up the one Kenneth had carried in earlier and looked inside. The sprigged muslin was stuffed into it. She took the whole thing upstairs to the office, transferred the cloth-wrapped hammer into the basket, and placed it in a dark corner behind the desk.

Bobby was standing in the door to the library, hands on hips, looking glum. The glamorous golden retriever had settled at his feet, lounging luxuriously and looking quite smug, as though she knew she'd fallen into a good thing.

"Bobby, did you see anyone unlikely about the house today? Someone who had no real business here? Getting off the elevator on this floor perhaps?"

Bobby said, "Not a soul. I think almost everyone's gone. My precious girl would have noticed anyone wandering the halls. She certainly noticed Godfrey's beast sniffing about. I think he may still be here. What am I going to do, Margaret?"

"What's wrong? You don't look happy."

"The spark has left me. Gloria's gone, and they've made the wood just a touch too dark. I can't face having it redone." He shrugged wearily "But I will. Perfection is my middle name. Poor Gloria." Margaret thought for a moment that he was going to weep. "She was so good to everyone, me especially. I hope Anton has the decency to arrange a lovely memorial service for her. Unless he did it. I wouldn't put anything past him. I guess he stands to inherit quite a lot, as will her children."

"I wonder if she made provision for Dougie," Margaret said, "or her former husband, from whom a lot of her money came."

Bobby grimaced. "It seems unlikely. Even darling

Gloria knew Dougie is a perfectly dreadful person. And she'd never give Angela the satisfaction. I'd love to pin murder on Dougie."

"It may yet be possible," Margaret said, and looked at her watch. "I wonder if I have time to do my chore for Giovanni."

"You could have come to work for me, you know," Bobby said. "Although I don't have the resources John has, so I probably couldn't afford you. I am, however, a much better designer than he is, for all his Italian make-believe. He only changed his name so people would speak of him in the same breath as Mario Buatta, John Saladino, and Vince Lattuca Donghia. The legendary Italian touch."

"I do have to run," Margaret said, and ran. But she checked the ground floor and the basement before she left, to no avail. The elevator had settled there again. Dougie had put away his cue and departed. Suddenly Margaret heard a sound in the old, darkened kitchen behind her.

She did not choose to face a possibly murderous person again, so she called out, "I'm coming just now, Bobby. Do you have your dog on a lead?"

The dog in question, however, was Daisy, who lifted her impressive muzzle in Margaret's direction and took a few tentative, ungainly steps toward her.

"Come along," Margaret said. "We can't have you roaming about on your own." Daisy trotted after her as she headed up to the first floor, where Godfrey's dining room looked near completion, especially when Daisy heaved herself down under the table, worn out by her venture into the basement.

Alfred had painted his entrance area just outside the

dining room a rich, glossy red. The boy was no longer on guard at the front door, so Margaret let herself out and hailed a cab to take her to the gallery. As she settled back in the seat she wondered how she was going to explain this day to De Vere.

She already had a good idea what he would say in response. She only hoped he wouldn't choose the moment for a final break.

Chapter 17

*T*he gallery was clean, white, and spare, as was Carl, the person Giovanni had told her to see. Carl ushered her into another white room, lined with cabinets with long, shallow, flat drawers. A few eye-catching and colorful Miró and Braque lithographs hung on the walls to relieve the relentless whiteness.

Carl sat her down in a comfortable executive chair with a broad table at just the right height, and started pulling portfolios of photographs from the drawers and laying them out on the table so they could leaf through them together. Carl pulled up another chair and opened the first volume.

Diane Arbus. Her oddities didn't seem right for Giovanni's room. They were strange people, ugly many of them, and some of them nearly freaks.

"I think not," Margaret said cautiously. Arbus was something of an icon, and one didn't want to sound unappreciative. "Giovanni mentioned Gary Winogrand. . . ."

"What a talent," Carl said, and brushed back a recalcitrant wave of blond hair from his forehead. "Witty, able to capture true moments of real life. A wonderful photographer. Unfortunately, we don't represent him. I think we may have one or two, but here's someone whose work you might like." Carl fetched another portfolio. "Younger, but with a sensibility similar to Gary's. Ready to capture the genuine moments. The faces, the dramatic instant, the truth. Take a look at these."

She looked and was enchanted. There were proud matrons walking tiny dogs, children mimicking the expression of animals at the zoo, groups of dangerous-looking street youths gazing sullenly at the camera, photos of typical New York mob scenes at Central Park rallies and street fairs. She was charmed by a picture of a little girl who had dropped her ice-cream cone and was witnessing it being crushed under the foot of a very large man. The man's expression was equally dismayed.

There were shots of weary, excited, disappointed faces at a political convention seen against a background of balloons and banners. Finally, there were slick, macho guys in dinner jackets apparently at a nightclub, surrounded by overdressed, overly made-up party girls. Martini glasses on the table and ashtrays with curls of smoke rising from them.

She opened another portfolio. St. Patrick's Cathedral on Fifth Avenue on a summer's day. The photographer had obviously staked out the church during the wedding season, for here were shots of brides arriving in Central Park's horse-drawn carriages, or monstrous white stretch limos, angelic flower girls in bouffant dresses, and little boy ring bearers, dressed to the nines, with a look of devilry in their faces as they watched the wedding party assemble. Solemn fathers, uncomfortable in tails, bridesmaids primping on the steps in front of the cathedral's great doors. Finally, the newlyweds emerging from the church, surrounded by the guests with the priest smiling benevolently on his handiwork.

The last photo in the portfolio gave her pause: two brides facing each other on the steps. One bride was nonchalantly adjusting her bodice while the other glared at her, her face distorted by rage, hands on hips, while someone—her mother perhaps—arranged her long white satin train.

"That's one of my favorites," Carl said, looking over her shoulder. "What a story it tells. He took thousands of pictures of weddings, just on his own, not as the official photographer. He's still taking them." He shook his head, as if to say, "Marriage, indeed." He made a move to collect the portfolio, but Margaret held on to it, still gazing at the two brides.

"Exactly what story, I wonder," she said.

"He's done country weddings and city weddings," Carl said. "He even did a series in Rome, with all these wonderful Roman matrons standing up proud and disdainful in front of some fabulous Renaissance churches. He's shot all around the world—Europe, Japan, even India—although I don't think black-and-white can do justice to a bride who's dressed in red."

Margaret was still staring at the two confrontational brides. She frowned. "I wonder . . . Two brides. How many grooms were there, do you suppose? The usual two, or were they sharing just the one?" She tapped the photo in its protective sleeve with a well-manicured nail. "They couldn't have both married the same . . ." She stopped. "I think we'd like this one for the showhouse."

"Whatever you want," Carl said. "Whatever Giovanni wants."

Margaret leafed through several portfolios and chose half a dozen more photographs, ever mindful of the grayness of the planned room. Then she returned to the photo of the two brides once more. "It would make a diverting story if both women had married the same man. Some sort of mix-up. I guess the first one down the aisle would be the true wife."

"And the husband would be a bigamist," Carl said as he gathered up the portfolios to return them to their drawers. "We'll get these framed and over to the show-house in a few days. Soon enough?"

"I should think so," Margaret said. "The decorators are in the thick of it, but it looks like a long process. I don't think Giovanni will get around to hanging pictures anytime soon. But he'll want his decorative objects at hand so when the moment of inspiration strikes, he'll be ready."

"I understand," Carl said. "Let me give you our card so the credit in the journal will be spelled correctly. You will see that the photos are returned to us when they tear down the rooms."

"Certainly," Margaret said. "I do hope no one walks off with any of them."

"In that event," Carl said cheerfully "Giovanni will get a hefty bill. In fact, we'll put an invoice with the framed photos when we deliver them. That way you'll know what they're worth for insurance purposes and in case of petty theft. But since they're definitely not cheap, the theft would be more on the level of grand. I say, you're quite taken with that bridal shot, aren't you."

"It answers a question," Margaret said.

"What question?"

"Whodunit. I think. I must rush. Thanks awfully for your help."

Margaret paused on the street outside the gallery to call Poppy. "I must see Hannah before she leaves," she said. "Is she there?"

"Certainly not."

"If you speak to her, suggest that she be careful. You, too."

"I don't understand."

"I think you do, Poppy. Blackmail is dangerous."

"But I don't know that I can locate Hannah on such short notice. I don't know where she's stopping. She calls me. Gloria knew, but she's . . . gone." Poppy managed to sound as though she was reporting the death of Bambi's mother.

"I know where she is, and so does Dougie," Margaret said, mostly to herself.

"Dougie, of course," Poppy said. "Hannah mentioned they'd met during this visit. She . . . she had some business with him."

"I'm sure she did," Margaret said.

Wearily, Margaret headed home to prepare for dinner with De Vere, during which she'd have to tell him about the hidden hammer and the unexpected, although harmless attack on her at the showhouse.

She stopped at a Gristede's supermarket and picked up some real Ben & Jerry's Cherry Garcia ice cream. No yogurt, no fat-free stuff. She bought some chocolate for good measure.

She stopped in the midst of receiving change from the checkout girl.

"Ma'am?" the girl said nervously. She had stupendously decorated long fingernails and elaborately braided and beaded hair, although Margaret was too deep in her own thoughts to notice. "The customers . . ."

Margaret looked behind her and saw that the line was becoming restive and could easily turn ugly if she didn't move along.

"What? Oh, sorry." She gathered up her bag of ice cream and departed.

The first thing she did when she got to her apartment and started her bath running was to call the Villa d'Este. Hannah Garber was registered there, and answered after several rings.

"Margaret Priam here. I . . . I need to speak with you on a matter of considerable urgency."

"You are speaking with me," Hannah said.

"I'd prefer a face-to-face meeting," Margaret said. "I could be with you in twenty minutes."

"If you wish," Hannah said reluctantly. "I have an engagement early this evening. Also of considerable urgency."

"Dougie, I suppose."

She didn't deny it. "Is it true what Dougie tells me? That Gloria is dead?"

"Murdered," Margaret said. "I will be there shortly."

She turned off the water flowing into the bathtub. She shrugged and allowed the warm, scented water to drain away. If she hurried, she could take care of her business with Hannah and get back for a long, soothing bath before dinner.

Hannah Garber greeted her without much warmth in the sitting room of her suite at the d'Este. She was wearing a green satin lounging robe, almost the same color as the fabric Gloria had found at the house.

"Is this a little foray into irony?" Margaret asked, eyeing the robe.

Hannah looked at her blankly.

"The color, the fabric . . ." Margaret said.

"I don't like riddles," Hannah said.

"Or jokes presumably," Margaret said. "Never mind. It wasn't a riddle, merely a test, and you passed it." Hannah apparently did not recognize the connection between her robe and the scene of Gloria's fall.

"What is it you want of me?" Hannah asked.

"I've concluded that Gloria Anton's death is related to what transpired between you and Dougie Gilpin all these years ago, and the part you both played—"

"In Eric's death?" Hannah laughed hollowly. "I've already told you I had nothing to do with that. It was all Dougie's doing. He wanted to scare Eric to keep him from tattling to his elders about matters which were best kept private."

"Your marriage. Your thefts."

Hannah rubbed her hands together nervously. "They were mistakes, made a long time ago."

"But you did trick Dougie into marrying you by telling him you were expecting his child."

Hannah waved that away. "Men are so easy to manipulate. And maybe I thought I *was* pregnant. There weren't many alternatives back then outside of marriage."

"But you then ran off with René Crouzat and married him. Did he think it was his child, too?"

"There was no child," Hannah said.

"But did you ever terminate your marriage to Dougie?"

"René didn't care. And we didn't actually get married, you know. He just wanted to get away from New York, and so did I. For different reasons. He wanted to try his hand at seducing little California girls, and I wanted to get away from the Gilpins. Old Douglas was rich, but he was making certain demands I didn't care to agree to. Dougie didn't dare leave or tell old Douglas about us out of fear of losing his inheritance. Of course, Poppy fixed that by telling Douglas things about Eric's death that I'd confided in her, and maybe even about the marriage. In any event, Dougie got a lot less than he expected."

"So you were still Mrs. Dougie when you left town. And I suspect you remain so to this day. And that presents Dougie with a real problem. As long as you were thousands of miles away, and asking only for some financial support, he didn't have to worry. But by coming back and talking to Gloria, you became a danger to him. I wonder why he didn't divorce you?"

"Dougie didn't think he had to follow anybody's silly laws. He got away with murder, after all. Not just Eric, but the girl up in Connecticut in the drunk-driving accident. He likes to think if he can't see it, it's not there."

"But now you're here, and he can't ignore the fact that he has two wives."

Margaret thought again of the photo of the two brides, the one indifferent and the other furious.

She closed her eyes, and saw again the person who had attacked her at the showhouse, and she understood what had been trying to reach her consciousness.

"I have to go home, Hannah. This will certainly become a police matter, and in any case, your blackmailing days are coming to an end."

Hannah shrugged. "It wasn't all that much that I got from Dougie, just a bit now and then for old time's sake. He told me that what he sent me he borrowed from Gloria." She sank down on the hotel-issue sofa. "I'm leaving tomorrow, and putting all this behind me. I'm not young anymore, but I do have a prospect or two back in California. Wealthy widowers who want a well-mannered lady to share their twilight years. I'll do all right."

"The police may want to talk to you."

"I have nothing to hide from them."

"Except for the fact that your marriage led to the death of two people."

"Eric yes, but it was his own fault. But two? I had nothing to do with Gloria's death."

"Yes," Margaret said. "Yes, you did."

Chapter 18

Margaret did not put geranium scent into her bath, as she did not wish to be reminded of the dining room of the showhouse. She chose gardenia, and allowed herself to sink down into the warm, fragrant bathwater, trying to banish any thoughts of murder or marriage.

She intended to explain everything to De Vere and let him handle what needed handling. She knew he'd be displeased, but she'd done what she thought best, and she had, after all, figured out who must have killed poor Gloria. Who had killed Eric, although undoubtedly no proof still existed.

She expected De Vere at eight, and at eight, the doorman rang her apartment. De Vere must have arrived. The doorman knew him well, and seldom bothered to announce him. She was ready. She had her nice porcelain rice bowls set out, and the red lacquered chopsticks. Real hot mustard she'd made herself, a dish of plum sauce. She could never eat Chinese take-out food without remembering how dangerous it could be for the deliverymen, but De Vere would arrive safely.

It seemed to be taking him far too long to reach her apartment from the lobby. She listened at the door for any sound, but heard nothing. Finally, her impatience got the better of her, and she opened the door to take a look down the hall in the direction of the elevators.

"Oh!" Margaret gasped and stepped back.

Pauline Gilpin forced her way into the apartment, grasping Margaret's arm in a very powerful grip.

"Pauline, what on earth . . . ?"

"You know everything."

Margaret had not expected a confrontation of this nature. "Yes," she said. "But I haven't told anyone. I mean, about Dougie and Eric."

"That." Pauline spit out the word contemptuously. "Nobody could ever prove anything about that. I'm talking about *me*." She was still holding Margaret's arm tightly, and her face was close to Margaret's.

"I know you attacked me at the showhouse, to keep me from finding the hammer you used to strike Gloria."

"You can't prove that either. No one saw me, not even Dougie when I passed him in the basement."

"But if you had a good enough motive," Margaret said, "someone could piece things together, and come up with you."

"I doubt it."

"Yet you were sufficiently unsure that you had to kill Gloria, who'd learned that Dougie is still married to Hannah Garber. Hannah herself told her. A bigamist. I'm not sure about the law, but the scandal would be the delight of social New York."

"I've taken legal advice. It would have been settled without fuss, but you're right. Gloria hated Dougie, and she would have loved to cause him as much trouble as possible. And she was going to tell about

Eric. She remembered seeing someone up on the fourth floor when Eric fell. Then she claimed just a few days ago at the luncheon that she actually saw Dougie push him. She told me herself, and I couldn't let her start telling everyone else. Dougie's all I have. He may not be the best man in the world, but I wasn't going to allow him to be held up to ridicule. Or me, for that matter."

"I don't know why you didn't just go after Hannah. That would rid you of all your problems."

"She's next," Pauline said. "After you." She was fumbling to reach into the large shoulder bag she carried. Margaret tried to pull away from her grip, but she seemed unusually strong.

"I work out a lot," Pauline said. "My instructor at the health club has remarked on the strength I've developed. I don't think you can break my hold. And I actually have a gun in my bag, and I've taken quite a few lessons, so I know how to use it."

"I don't doubt you for a minute," Margaret said, and experienced a sense of overwhelming relief to see De Vere standing in the doorway, observing the scene with a mildly bemused expression.

"Sorry to be late," he said. "They ran out of lobster, and I had to wait while they fetched some more. Am I interrupting some girlish play?"

At least Pauline ceased to rummage through her bag for the alleged gun she carried. She turned and smiled graciously to De Vere. "Hello, I'm Pauline Gilpin. Margaret and I were just testing to see who had achieved more from our daily workouts at the gym."

De Vere laughed. "Now, that's not true, dear lady. I

don't believe anyone could pay Margaret enough just to set foot in a place where one worked out."

At that, Pauline finally released Margaret's arm.

"She came here to kill me," Margaret said. "She's already killed her sister-in-law, Gloria Anton. There's a hammer she used on the fourth floor of the Gilpin house, behind an old desk, in a wicker basket."

"What nonsense," Pauline said.

"No," Margaret said. "I found it in the steamer trunk and I hid it. Do something, Sam."

"All right, but I don't want the food to get cold. Lobster is expensive. Both of you sit while I make a call."

"Leave your bag here," Margaret said to Pauline, "in case you feel the need to take out your gun."

"Gun? I don't have a gun."

"Nevertheless . . ." Margaret said. Pauline sat, leaving her bag beside Margaret, who gingerly retrieved a small gun from it. She knew enough about guns to see that it was loaded.

"Everyone carries guns nowadays," Pauline said. "And I don't know by what authority you're keeping me here."

"Mr. De Vere is with the police," Margaret said, "and you did threaten me." De Vere looked over from the phone and saw that Margaret was holding the gun. He grimaced.

"I see," Pauline said, and stood up. "I will be available at my home." She moved quickly and was out the door. De Vere hung up and went after her, while Margaret, knowing what was really important, gathered up the bags of take-out food De Vere had brought and took them to the kitchen. De Vere was back in a few moments.

"There was an elevator just arriving on this floor," he said. "She was in it and away before I could stop her, not that I had a reason to. Why don't you put that gun away and tell me what this is about, before I do something foolish and cause the department no end of trouble."

"It's her gun. Sit down," she said. "You're not going to believe this."

"Get the food, and I'll do my best," he said, and smiled wryly. "I was kind of hoping for a quiet evening at home with my best friend."

It took Margaret quite a long time to explain, step by step, what had happened in the Gilpin family over the course of four decades, and especially what had happened over the past few days.

She found the sad tale of death, suicide, and unhappy marriages quite affecting, but it did not stop her from selecting succulent chunks of lobster meat dripping with garlicky sauce and savoring the texture and spice of the perfect dry sautéed crispy beef. De Vere, who had heard many an unhappy story in his time, did not appear to be greatly moved.

"Lovely food," Margaret said, licking a drop of garlic sauce from a finger. "Well, finally Pauline was so desperate to keep Gloria from telling people about Hannah and Dougie's unterminated marriage, and worse, about Dougie pushing his brother down the stairs, that she must have started haunting the house to learn her way about. Dougie may have had the key from the old days, and they seemed to be quite lackadaisical about locking up. Bobby Henley was there late one night all alone and heard someone come in. Anyhow, Pauline lifted the construction man's hammer during one of her visits as a committee member, and waited for the right moment. The wrong moment for Gloria."

De Vere said, "I wonder if any of this is provable."

"The hammer . . . and Pauline came for me. There's the gun."

"It's something, but since you moved the hammer about . . . I've notified people to keep the house secure. No one in until tomorrow. There's a sort of evidential case against Pauline. I'll tell people to keep an eye on her. She can probably muster a hundred lawyers. Are you sure about all this?"

"If not Pauline, there are others. . . . Peter Anton? He needs Gloria's money, as does Dougie." She pushed away her rice bowl and put down her chopsticks. "Marriage, in this context at least, appears to be an appalling adventure."

"Do you think so?" De Vere cocked his head and gazed at her. "My experience wasn't a success, but the circumstances were difficult."

"Look at all these Gilpins. No success there either, except maybe Gloria's daughter. The circumstances of the older generation haven't been difficult, but their marriages have resulted in a number of deaths."

"They weren't marrying for love, but rather for stocks and bonds. If what you're telling me is true, it was marriage for the sake of money, status, freedom, and lots of other stuff except what the real thing is supposed to be about. The idea that 'I accept the way you are, you accept me, and we'll take on the enterprise together.' "

Margaret looked at him as he directed his chopsticks to the large remaining lobster claw.

"Let's try that approach, then. Who I am is someone inviting you to accompany me to the gala opening of the SPDA designer showhouse, early in May. You have plenty of time to think it over, a couple of months."

"It sounds perfectly awful," De Vere said, and smiled. "I accept the invitation, and who you are. I don't want it to end. Ever."

"I understand," Margaret said. "It's what I want, too."

"As long as the galas are kept to a minimum, and Chinese feasts are a regular feature of our life together."

"And Cherry Garcia," Margaret said. "I love you, Sam."

"Likewise. Where's the ice cream?"

Chapter 19

The warm May night was perfect for the opening of the SPDA designer showhouse. In two months, the decorators had achieved marvelous effects, and had not killed each other. The two dogs had found true companionship, and except for one distressing incident involving a leather box, which had graced "A Gentleman's Study," that had somehow been chewed beyond redemption or recognition, they had not caused many problems.

For the gala opening, De Vere had reluctantly succumbed to the necessity of wearing black tie and looked impressive as he mounted the steps from the street with Margaret on his arm. They were met at the door by, of all people, Eddie Leone, similarly garbed, but unlike De Vere, ill at ease in his finery. Eddie had been separated from Margaret for some weeks by the rush of events, but was quickly aglow at the sight of her. He managed one dark scowl at De Vere, and was then emboldened to embrace Margaret as though they were intimates of long standing. Eddie must have been observing the air-kissing rituals of the showhouse crowd.

"How nice to see you again, Eddie," Margaret

said. "This is Sam De Vere." The men shook hands warily, and De Vere said, "I believe we met during our investigation."

"It ain't been easy, Lady Margaret, I can tell you," Eddie said, reluctant to look De Vere in the eye. "The boss was real broken up when the missus died that way. And to think they're saying Mrs. Dougie did it. I guess she was nuts or something."

"I heard," Margaret said. "Mr. De Vere is with the police, so I've been kept informed." Of course, her true informants were people like Poppy and Dianne. De Vere, even though her future husband, was not one to share gossip, official or otherwise. What the ladies were saying, however, was that Pauline and Dougie had hired an army of lawyers, Pauline had not been formally accused, and everybody thought she was going to get away with it.

At the word *police* Eddie found he had important duties to attend to, as groups of decorators, committee women and escorts, and paying gala goers were arriving.

Inside, the cheery bright red foyer was crowded with well-dressed lovers of fine interior design. Dianne waved from across the space, and Terry Thompson, who had abandoned red hair for a distinguished tawny brown, stepped forward in a stately manner.

"It's all going perfectly," she said. "The doors open to the public tomorrow at ten, and we've gotten a lot of notice in the press, thanks to Gloria's mishap. It's going to be wonderful!"

Margaret looked at her sharply.

"Here's Madame Ambassador with a bunch of other excellencies," Terry said out of the corner of her mouth. "I don't imagine anything in the house is quite to the taste of even a very wealthy African, but you never know."

"Aha!" Margaret said as Godfrey Helms marched in with the enormous Daisy in what looked to be a rhinestone collar. Daisy had the good sense to draw back in dismay at the profusion of gowns and jewels, although she lifted her head pleadingly at the sight of a waiter with a tray of stuffed mushrooms and tiny quail's eggs heaped with caviar. Margaret took a quail's egg.

Daisy sat down heavily, with a haughty expression, as the waiter passed her by. Her eyes seemed to say, "My ancestors were gamboling across the peat bogs with the high kings of Ireland while yours were learning to press olive oil and grind corn."

"It's all right, old girl," Godfrey said. "I'll find you a snack before the night is done." He didn't notice Margaret slip her delicacy to an eager Daisy.

Daisy swallowed politely and seemed to grin. "Good dog," Margaret said. Daisy moved over and leaned against her.

"Have you seen the house, Margaret?" Godfrey asked.

"I was about to set off upstairs," she said.

"Come look at my dining room. It's an absolute dream."

De Vere appeared to be deep in conversation with Charlie Stark, so Margaret allowed Godfrey to pull her by the hand to his room. As they neared it she heard the faint sounds of Gregorian chant. Surely it must be a recording, since the row of cowled figures seated at the long table did not seem to be singing.

"Godfrey, I never dreamed you'd actually—"

"Only for tonight, darling," he said. "It's far too expensive to keep them for every day. There are all sorts of rules."

"Surely they're not . . . not real."

"Real? Oh, you mean, real *monks*. No, that entails even more rules. These are merely union people."

"Did Bobby get his person to sit upstairs with his dog?"

"Quite a cute number," Godfrey said coldly. "Well, what do you think of my room?"

Margaret gazed upward to the gorgeous, glittering crystal chandelier that shimmered faint rainbows. Fortunately, it had electric bulbs rather than black candles to drip on the patient monks seated below it. The geranium walls did seem to work, and the suggestion of a sunset beyond the faux window was believable.

"It's lovely, Godfrey. Gracious and comfortable and—"

"I know, a bit too clerical."

"I'd like to see the kitchen." Margaret trailed through the room to the much-disputed door. Stacy and Lacy had created a charming blue-and-white room, with a vast range and refrigerator on one side, butcher-block counters, and a wall of cabinets. There were blue-and-white-striped curtains, a wooden table painted deep blue set for breakfast, with pots of yellow tulips on table and shelves.

"Where are the kitchen ladies?" Margaret asked.

"My dear, they are circulating and they are actually wearing dresses. We've gotten to be quite chummy, since they've completely taken over management of Daisy. How I ever let Bobby talk me into having a dog . . ." Daisy raised her head and looked at him piteously. "Oh, all right. Good dog." Margaret patted her head. Daisy seemed content. Margaret left Godfrey to find De Vere, who was still deep in conversation with Charlie in the red foyer. She did catch his eye when they both noticed Pauline and Dougie entering the house. Pauline held her head high, and Dougie beamed genially at everyone.

"What brass," Dianne murmured into Margaret's ear. "I suppose we'll be seeing Peter Anton any second now, and even Angela. All the people who wished Gloria dead among all of us who mourn her. Oh, she had her faults. . . ."

Bobby joined them. "Gloria might have been bossy, but she had style, kindness, and she knew how to spend her money. And she knew the audience—people who want a glimpse of the surroundings needed to live an impossibly good life. I—and the other decorators—know how to create rooms that everyone wants to live and die in. It takes a Gloria Gilpin to put it together—not that Terry hasn't worked hard. But the very idea that Pauline would show up here. She's claiming all over town that she couldn't possibly have done it, it's all a plot Margaret manufactured to drive her insane."

"More likely, as Poppy remarked, Hannah drove Pauline 'round the bend with her blackmail threats," Margaret said. "I know what she tried to do to me. At least she hasn't tried it again. And the police found the hammer, and they know about Dougie's bigamous activities, although Miss Hannah has vanished in a cloud of Joy." She sighed. "Let's take a look at the rest of the house. Bobby can do the honors for his room."

Pauline pointedly ignored Margaret as she, Bobby, and Dianne passed her on their way upstairs to the library.

"Bobby, it's sensational!" Margaret had seen the room's progress over the past few weeks when she had come in to assist Giovanni, but here it was in perfect shape. The rich, dark wood of the wainscoting reflected subdued light from a green-shaded lamp on the desk, dark green drapes covered the windows, and the silky blond retriever was curled up on a round puffy red pillow on the dark green carpet in front of the fireplace. Bobby had filled the bookshelves with leather-bound, gold-stamped volumes, one of which was in the hands of a tall young man, one of the handsomest Margaret had ever seen. His painfully WASPish dressing gown could only be from Ralph Lauren, his tan from St. Bart's, and his poise from the stage.

"A Traditional Library," he intoned. "Please do not fondle the dog. Mr. Henley's cards are on the desk, if you wish to contact—"

"It's okay, Josh," Bobby said. "But you do a great job. Say, Margaret, if it's true what I hear about you getting married, I could do a room like this for you as a wedding present. I never figured you for the marrying kind."

Margaret laughed. "I wonder if I am. He's a wonderful person, and it seems that we belong together. He's downstairs. You'll meet him later when he comes up."

"He won't approve of me," Bobby said.

"Unless he encounters you in the commission of a crime, Sam De Vere is pretty open to just about everyone."

She peered out the door. "Lots of folks on their way up." Josh straightened the lapels of his robe and seated himself in the leather armchair. The dog wandered over and put her head on his knee, as if on cue. Josh opened his book. Margaret wondered if anyone that handsome had actually mastered reading.

"Candy, how delightful to see you." Bobby was in his element. "And Susanna darling, come right in. . . . Ah, Angela . . ."

Margaret and Dianne whipped around to see Angela Forsythe glide into Bobby's room.

"Terry begged me to come," Angela said. "I wouldn't miss it for anything." She said to Margaret, "I have a perfect right to be here, it's a public event. Bobby, you've done wonders since Pauline showed me this room. Is that dog friendly? Dogs make me nervous." She stepped back as the retriever raised its muzzle.

"Pauline?" Margaret interrupted.

"We're old friends," Angela said, narrowing her eyes. "She told me all about how Gloria tried to smash her marriage with vile rumors, and you haven't helped with your stupid accusations. Gloria devoted herself to spoiling my life with Leland, so she deserved everything she got."

"Angela, this isn't really the time or place. . . ."

Suddenly the commanding voice of Madame Ambassador summoned the viewers to her "Lady's Retreat," and Margaret sought the haven of Giovanni's strangely comforting gray, black, and white room that had once been the music room. The pictures she'd chosen looked elegant on the walls above a long black leather sofa. She smiled again at the sight of the disputing brides, the ones she'd imagined were Hannah and Pauline arguing over Dougie. She looked again: they could as easily be Gloria and Angela facing off over Leland Forsythe.

Unsettled, she strolled around Giovanni's room. She

knew it well, since she'd followed its progress. There were the audiovisual systems he loved, with hidden controls, and a television set that rose from a pedestal in the middle of the room, and turned to face any viewer with a remote control that also dimmed and raised the lights, opened the curtains, turned on the stereo, and indeed answered the telephone. Giovanni hadn't opted for clutter. The room was almost Japanese in its simplicity. A black-lacquered tree branch in a turquoise ceramic pot stood in one corner, a jagged ice-blue chunk of glass like an Alp shooting out glints of prismatic color sat on a low table made of glass and black wood. The rug was slate-colored, the walls a strange off-white with a tinge of gray. A filmy turquoise scarf exactly the color of the ceramic pot had been tossed over the arm of the sofa. Diffused light came from behind a three-panel standing screen.

"Interesting," Dianne said. She'd followed Margaret into Giovanni's room. "But I want to see what Madame Ambassador has done. I've almost persuaded Charlie to hire her to redo our place. She's frightfully expensive, but it's the look Charlie likes. This room is a little too dark for my taste, and his." Dianne wandered off to view silk walls and lush canopied beds.

Margaret sat on the sofa and watched people pass the open door seeking out ever-more-extravagant decorating fancies. There went Juana de los Angeles, tricked out in a mauve gown to match her room. Terry Thompson led a flock of committee ladies upward and onward. Margaret closed her eyes. Giovanni had placed baskets of potpourri behind the screen so that the room was faintly scented. Margaret hoped De Vere was being entertained. She closed her eyes and almost dozed off.

The sound of the door shutting roused her immediately. She could make out someone standing there, back to the closed door.

"Who is it?" But she was certain it was Angela Forsythe.

"She could have had the decency to return Leland's money. She could have put something in her will," Angela hissed. "I expected it. The children would have had plenty in any case."

"Angela, what *is* your problem?" Margaret stood up.

"You are, getting Pauline into trouble that way. She's my friend. And she had every reason to loathe Gloria, almost as much as I did. I helped her in every way I could."

"Namely?"

"I helped her steal the hammer, I told her all about how Eric had died so Gloria's fall would seem the same." Angela moved slowly across the room toward the sofa.

Margaret watched her as she neared the low table with the jagged glass mountain, and thought she didn't like the look on Angela's face. Marriage and money had apparently driven all these women mad. She was beginning to wonder about her chances for success with De Vere.

Margaret stood up suddenly as Angela reached out to grasp the block of glass.

"A cozy conspiracy, was it?" Margaret said. "You and Pauline?" Angela withdrew her hand quickly. Margaret waved toward the picture of the two brides above the sofa. "Too many brides, too few husbands, so the extra wives banded together to get rid of the thorn in their sides, who had too many tales to tell. Poor Gloria."

Angela edged again toward the heavy piece of glass, but Margaret was unwilling to be the object of a bashing. There had been too many already. She wasn't sure, however, that she could physically best a woman who devotedly worked out at her gym. As Angela raised the lethal object Margaret saw the door being pushed open. Pauline appeared. Two strong women were two more than she felt she could handle.

"Angela, don't be stupid," Pauline said. "We can't get away with it with so many people about. You should have picked a place like the fourth floor, where no one was around to see me hit Gloria and send her down the stairs trailing that green satin."

Margaret held her breath as Pauline picked up the scarf from the sofa. "But if we can't silence Margaret one way, we'll try another, put her behind the screen, and get ourselves to Bobby's room or downstairs. No one will be able to place us here."

Now Margaret saw that the door was being pushed open by a large squarish, hairy nose.

"Good dog!" she said enthusiastically. Angela and Pauline hesitated, and Daisy lumbered in, looking especially large in the dim lighting. Daisy proceeded toward Margaret while the women backed off.

"Mind the dog," Margaret said, holding onto Daisy's collar and edging toward the door. "She's trained to kill." Daisy accepted the slander, and they backed out of the room.

"Oh, hullo!" She bumped into De Vere, who was standing outside with Charlie Stark.

"Hello yourself," De Vere said. "I was looking for you. When I heard your voice in there . . . well, Charlie and I have been eavesdropping. Interesting conversation, although I don't know what it will mean for Mrs. Gilpin and Mrs. Forsythe. At least things have fallen into place in my mind. I suppose I'll have to go in there and talk to them." Daisy snuffled around Sam's nicely polished dress shoes. He eyed her warily as Godfrey and another man strolled along the landing in their direction.

"Sam, how do you feel about dogs?" Margaret was feeling especially affectionate toward Daisy.

"This thing? I doubt it's a dog at all. . . ."

"Not a 'thing,' my good man," Godfrey said. "A marvelous beast. I wondered where she'd gotten to. The monks feel there's something missing without her. That regal touch that pulls my room together."

"She is an empress among dogs," Margaret said, and scratched the wiry fur on Daisy's head.

Godfrey said, "I don't believe you've met Leland Forsythe."

"Mr. Forsythe," Margaret said. "I was just . . . talking to your wife."

"I'm looking for her," Leland said. "I can't seem to keep up with her."

"I believe she and Pauline Gilpin are admiring this room," Margaret said, and indicated the closed door to Giovanni's room.

"I won't bring her out until Godfrey takes the dog away," Leland said. "She doesn't care for dogs."

"I see," Margaret said, and looked down at Daisy. "Good dog."

The well-heeled, well-adjusted Lady Margaret Priam wishes her other well-to-do friends had better luck. For example, it would be nice if they could stay alive.

But then, what would she do for amusement?

The Lady Margaret Priam mysteries
by Joyce Christmas

SUDDENLY IN HER SORBET
A FÊTE WORSE THAN DEATH
A STUNNING WAY TO DIE
FRIEND OR FAUX
IT'S HER FUNERAL
A PERFECT DAY FOR DYING

Murder is *so* gauche.

But, Lady Margaret Priam must admit, it
will never be passé.

The Lady Margaret
Priam mysteries

Available at your local bookstore.
Published by Fawcett Books.